PENGUIN BOOKS
DON'T ASK ANY OLD BLOKE FOR DIRECTIONS

P.G. Tenzing studied at Delhi University. He was in the Kerala cadre of the Indian Administrative Service for twenty years. His colleagues said of him, as he embarked on his adventures: 'Philosopher, eccentric, drinking companion, fitness freak, party animal, secret workaholic, visiting professor, reluctant officer, successful hotelier and great friend of all.'

Don't Ask Any Old Bloke for Directions

A Biker's Whimsical Journey across India

P.G. TENZING

PENGUIN BOOKS

PENGUIN BOOKS
Published by the Penguin Group
Penguin Books India Pvt. Ltd, 11 Community Centre, Panchsheel Park,
New Delhi 110 017, India
Penguin Group (USA) Inc., 375 Hudson Street, New York, New York 10014, USA
Penguin Group (Canada), 90 Eglinton Avenue East, Suite 700, Toronto,
Ontario, M4P 2Y3, Canada (a division of Pearson Penguin Canada Inc.)
Penguin Books Ltd, 80 Strand, London WC2R 0RL, England
Penguin Ireland, 25 St Stephen's Green, Dublin 2, Ireland
(a division of Penguin Books Ltd)
Penguin Group (Australia), 250 Camberwell Road, Camberwell,
Victoria 3124, Australia (a division of Pearson Australia Group Pty Ltd)
Penguin Group (NZ), 67 Apollo Drive, Rosedale, North Shore 0632,
New Zealand (a division of Pearson New Zealand Ltd)
Penguin Group (South Africa) (Pty) Ltd, 24 Sturdee Avenue, Rosebank,
Johannesburg 2196, South Africa

Penguin Books Ltd, Registered Offices: 80 Strand, London WC2R 0RL, England

First published by Penguin Books India 2009

Copyright © Palden Gyatso Tenzing 2009

All rights reserved

10 9 8 7 6 5 4 3 2 1

ISBN 9780143102991

Typeset in Bembo by SÜRYA, New Delhi
Printed at Pauls Press, New Delhi

'Living your dreams, instead of just dreaming them, is not without risk.'

—Wanda Rutkiewicz,
mountain climber (1943–92)

Prologue

It had been a year in my new pad in Thiruvananthapuram. I had just returned from a long sabbatical and was back with the government of Kerala as a secretary of the fisheries department. Not that I know anything about fish—except how to eat it. While grappling with those marine animals I had been put in charge, in addition, of the transport department. Well, I knew how to drive and therefore felt more confident around that.

That was my life. Spent in groping around areas I didn't know or care about. And having to deal with the vicious in-fighting that goes on inside every government I have ever served.

My minister, the fishy one, was a know-all and did not trust the bureaucracy. I didn't blame him, and so we worked together in uneasy harmony. I had decided to deal with him with Sphinx-like stolidity, my mouth tightly shut. I was so successful with this strategy that he had begun to request to hear my voice from time to time.

The transport guy, on the other hand, relied completely on us, since he was from a minor party and had no back-up. I liked him.

The family was back home in Sikkim. I lived with my Jeeves, an adivasi from north Bengal. He cooked fish well.

My bedroom had a full-length mirror supplied by my narcissist landlord, and I had got into the habit of looking at myself after a bath, in the nude. Which was twice a day in this hot, humid climate. I saw the slide down southwards of my once trim body. The bulging waistline and the love handles too terrible to behold with equanimity. Worse, I suspected I would soon need a bra. (Would that come under medical expenses?)

Depressed anew, early in the morning and again late at night, with the state of my body—and of course my mind—I began to question the rationale of going on as I was. I'd had plans before to leave the government service, but not the guts. I'd cocked the gun, but my finger lingered on the trigger.

And then, they dumped the last straw, the department of information technology, onto my back, on top of the other two. This was a high-profile post, much in view of the press. A high-profile ass is what I'd become.

So, naturally, I handed in my papers.

At the ripe old age of forty-three, I went for the idea I'd been pussyfooting around for almost a decade. I grabbed that star and waited to see if it pulled me up to the sky, or burnt me to cinders. At least, I reassured myself, I will have scratched that itch.

I had always wanted to travel at random and with only myself for company. I read somewhere that the only people who travel alone are the bad 'uns. Maybe. But I wanted to wander alone for a year, without a plan to cohere to. And I wanted to make that journey on that 350-cc king of the road. Watching my hair grow without combing it. Watching the sunrise and sunset from sea level and from the heights of the Himalayas. Getting my face burnt and my toes wet. Sweating and shivering. Crying and cowering. Laughing till I piss.

I made a blind leap into the void. And the freefall continues.

With a difference. Two self-appointed sleuths—one in journalism and another in publishing, the two professions I rate about as fearsome as the IAS—got wind of my plans. They waited to catch me drunk one evening and said, in a monumental effort to sound casual, 'Why don't you write about it all?'

I felt raped, plundered, ahead of the offence. This was to be *my* body of thought, I protested, *my* singular route to a crossroads I was yet to recognize. I didn't *care* if no one else saw it. If anything, I felt insanely possessive of it. 'So?' yawned the nosey-parkers in unison. 'It'll still be *your* trip.'

And so, as it turned out, it was.

1

So here I am, in a side lane in Delhi. The barber is taking
liberties with the straggly growth on my chin. He
nonchalantly lops a few strands from above my ears too.
I remember telling the fellow that I only wanted my beard
trimmed. Maybe my facial growth extends to beyond my
ears. Or maybe he is dissatisfied with the whole effect.
Whatever. I'm mesmerized with the fellow's antics. He
bellows something to somebody across the road. It's a fine
morning, 7.30 a.m., in a grotty alley in Delhi and I'm
sitting on a rickety chair under the sky and gazing at
myself in a mirror hung on some probably rickety VIP's
backyard wall.

Say hello to me. A retired bureaucrat. No. More
factually, a *voluntarily* retired bureaucrat. Age: Forty-three.
Sex: Occasionally. I was not pushed out of a trapdoor into
the abyss at the age of sixty. I leapt into the void as a
matter of choice. I have a streak of destructive energy in

me. Maybe I'm a little masochistic too, but the world loves a good drama and, anyway, the latest trend is suicide-bombing. Drama, a big bang, and gore everywhere. Voluntary retirement is a form of kamikaze too, only, in my case, there were no theatricals, no untoward noise, only a little puddle on the street. The one I left as I wet my pants jumping into the void.

Three months down the line, I'm jobless; I still have some pennies in my pocket and am getting a bad beard job done on me. The occasional haircut is gratis. Thanks to the kind, young vociferous barber. He is still on full volume to the chaiwallah across the street, obviously more interested in breaking his fast, having already broken my faith in his tradecraft. The cloth he's wrapped around my chest is a dirty ochre. I avert my eyes after one shy glance at the loathsome thing. These roadside barbers, a kind of deity, are notoriously touchy. They hate any suggestion that they are less than hygienic. They can easily ask you to take a hike and there are no doors to be opened and shut with a bang as a sign of protest after that. I swallow my aversion and submit to God and his scissors.

My notice to the Government of India that I planned to seek voluntary retirement was signed on 15 August 2006. No prizes for guessing why, unless you are an American.

One evening, I found myself feeding momos to Beni Ram, a *patwari* in Manali. We had met barely an hour before and no, we were not smashed on *pahari* dope. Yes, we had had a couple of large vodkas. No, we are not gay.

So, how can you explain a given set of actions on a particular day? Karma. Beni Ram owes me one now, because I surrendered my last momo to him. One day in the Indian Administrative Service (IAS), the next day out on the road. Karma. The concept of karma is one of the favourite whipping posts of the losers in the world. Let me add a few lashes to this comic cosmic drama.

It has been a meditative ride through the country. The rhythm of the road gets to you. Riding an Enfield has always been a one-of-a-kind pleasure for me. Having one between the legs for ten hours in a row is a pain in the ass, literally, but in a funny way, a long road journey is by itself a form of meditation. You have to be there in the moment. You cannot dream of the future or regurgitate the past for too long or you are liable to be 'ambulanced'. Your mind is spared quotidian cares, and gets the rest it so badly deserves.

I have fallen totally in love with the dirty, greasy beings we call mechanics. They are known as a breed of swindlers and charlatans but to my mind, no nobler creature exists in this world. In two different states of the country, three different mechanics did minor jobs on the motorcycle and each of them waved away the proffered money. They just liked the idea of the all-India drive that I'm on, or maybe I looked too poor to pay. My opinion of this breed of princes will remain the same till I find a real bastard among them. The karmic network tells me that I will find the bugger soon.

It was a good run in the IAS till I found that I was not

taking the job seriously and had started taking myself too seriously. That was taking the relationship between the job and myself on the negative foot and a bad human being will not make a good public servant. Time to call it quits. Thank you and goodbye. I'm still way too enamoured of myself, but the mechanics and the barbers and the dhaba-owners will see me through.

Somewhere in a dhaba in West Bengal, I went to irrigate the fields behind it and slipped and fell in a garbage heap. Not many people can imagine a dhaba's garbage heap, but let me tell you, it looks and smells worse than normal refuse. I had the pleasure of rubbing my President Bush on the noisome, squishy, multicoloured mess. The entire dhaba clan came to my rescue and I was hosed down with care on that extremely hot day. Thank God for the hot weather and the open motorcycle. The clothes were quickly dry except the area around President Bush. All this does wonders for chipping away at the stuffy old frog inside me.

'*Om Ah Hung Vajra Guru Padma Siddhi Hung*' is the root mantra of the Nyingmapa sect of Tibetan Buddhists, the one prevalent in Sikkim, where my home is. This is my constant prayer throughout the journey. There have been some nasty moments in the journey and I take refuge in the mantra. Even on good days and in good places, I recite the mantra in the hope that there is wisdom and compassion on other days and other places in the world. When I find myself staying put in a place long enough, I perform the puja called the Rewo Sang Cho, or the 'diamond practice'. This needs a special preparation of three white and three sweet substances, medicines, incense and associated stuff. This prolongs life and removes obstacles, particularly those associated with unpaid karmic debts. The whole point of this journey is to try and pay back unpaid karmic debts. A puja to help speed up the process is a bonus.

And what fun this is. Freedom to do as I please, stay where I want to and learn the things that matter.

2

I initially wanted to write this book in Manali, in Himachal Pradesh. I took a cottage there, which came with an unkempt garden. I even agreed to share the house with mice, insects and varieties of lizards. Then a black snake came to say hello and I said goodbye. Snakes are not my choice of live-in partners.

Now, nine months after I started my travels on my mobike, I find myself eyeballing the Annapurna range from a cottage near Begnas Lake, in Nepal. I am no longer alone. The caretaker Mohan and his family give me and my thirteen-year-old younger daughter, Dechen, our daily bread and some other rustic facilities. It is Mohan who is beginning to look like God to me now. Albeit a slightly malnourished and lazy God.

25,320 kilometres in nine months WITH SOME STOPS IN BETWEEN OR I WOULD HAVE DIED. The daily runs were anything between six to twelve hours. I drove slowly of course, my average speed around 40 kmph. Indian roads are for people with a death wish. I want to live a little bit longer. My motto during the ride was one coined by the Border Roads Organization: 'ALWAYS ALERT ACCIDENT AVERT'. Corny, but good enough for me.

This place that I finally landed in is weird, to say the least. The sun comes up only after the fog goes away— around ten in the morning. Till such time one lives in a cold haze, blanketed in a shroud of white every morning. Weather to make even a God lazy.

Dechen went out yesterday to a celebration of the Gurung New Year, and met a clouded leopard on the way. The way to greet a leopard around here is to scream bloody murder and run like hell. The cat eschews the screaming part but runs like hell in the other direction. So a foggy place with leopards in the yard and a stunning view with a lazy God in attendance is where my creative juices are supposed to flow. It's downright dangerous to use the outside toilet in the night and I threw myself with vigour into what I call the 'Balcony Ballet' since last night. At least that's flowing without a hitch.

25,320 kilometres. You've got to forgive me trumpeting the number. This is my drug for the time being. Being part of the Indian Administrative Service was my high for most part of my twenty years in service. Like any institution in the world, the IAS has its share of good, decent people and, unlike others, has maniacal creeps as the rest. During my time I generally managed to skirt the creeps using the famous Sikkimese Shuffle (a combination of charm, skill at intercepting moves, the use of leave options, and aggression, each in small doses.)

I faced a volley of objections from colleagues to my leaving the service. One cynic (an old fart, and I say this with respect), went as far as to question my resolve, even while holding my letter of resignation in his fist. He thought I was doing the Shuffle. A few months later, another Chief Secretary, a kindly old lady, asked me whether I'd changed my mind. Other advice and inducements awaited me: I should wait for the next pay commission, my imminent promotion as a central joint secretary, and the promise that my comparative youth held out, which would indicate I was meant to reach the highest echelons of the bureaucracy.

Compelling reasons, all, to a sane man. But when you've got a screw loose, you've got a screw loose.

Hey, this was not the act of a desperado. This was a well-thought-out exit strategy. To nowhere. The only immediate aim was to take time out for self. To be unashamedly selfish. To do my own thing. To answer to nobody. To not worry about love or money. To not look back—nor forward. To be here and now.

You can imagine the flood of events—the discussions with loved ones, the act of writing one's known life away, the final official acceptance of my bid for voluntary retirement, the benefits received, the plan to buy an Enfield . . . before the journey began.

3

I went to the showroom intending to buy the classic Enfield Bullet. But the canny salesman took me for a ride on the Thunderbird—and I was hooked. More stylish, more hi-tech (aluminum engine, et al), offering more mileage, more comfort and, of course, more expensive. Dark green, seguing into black and silver on the rest of the body. I added a small carrier to the back of my soul mate for the next nine months.

I had spent the majority of my service years in Kerala. What a beautiful state! What extraordinary people! What shitty politics!

The IAS fraternity gave me a cheery farewell. I had meals at various houses. Kuttapan, my dear friend and master of the keep-the-in-laws-at-bay-but-happy strategy, was constantly by my side. I rode out of the millennium apartments in Thiruvananthapuram on a fine March day to do the things I wanted to do.

First stop: Varkala beach resort. Only an hour's journey away. Holed up in Rajen's resort for a few days getting drunk with Suresh and company. Suresh is one of my oldest friends in Kerala, and a bundle of contradictions to boot. A great friend and a lousy enemy. A tortured soul sleeping with a variety of devils. Integrity beyond doubt. Ask me, I've often paid his bills. Great officer of the IAS but dearly misunderstood in his homeland. He has been my drinking buddy for decades. I could not say a proper goodbye to Kerala in a state of sobriety. *Cheers to Kerala*, I hollered, while weaving around the beaches of Varkala.

Then, in the throes of a staggering hangover, I started communion with my bike. The helmet, the boots, gloves, facemask and goggles were from good old Harley's outfit while the rucksack and the clothes and the knick-knacks were from humbler sources. It occurred to me that they were all the products of human minds and human hands I didn't know. Therein lay the sacred bond of humankind and everything in the universe. The place I was standing in, the places my journey would take me, even my particular intention in embarking on it, were the culmination of millions of forces, call them human, divine, of nature, due to destiny, or reasons that were plain loco.

There is a word, *Thamzi*, in the Bhutia language of Sikkim, which can loosely be translated as 'the sacred bond'. My understanding of this relationship is that it not only extends to human beings but to all that is sentient: the material world, the environment and the universe. Any interaction may be a fruit of your previous lives but how we carry forward that relationship is our choice. There is room for discretion on our part, and all is not ordained. I sent a heartfelt thank-you to all the forces that had brought me there.

And I also made a request to my bike. In fact, the bike was the focus of my requests. I don't know anything about mechanics; I don't know even how to change a tyre, for heaven's sake. I knew, vaguely, that I wanted to visit people and places, and that by my meeting them, they would, in turn, grow connected. The degrees of separation would decrease. The bike would choose some places for me, in its wisdom or, in other words, when it conked out. My request to the Thunderbird was to not fuck me up too much. Somehow, my fate was linked to the hands that made this bike, and I just hoped that ours was a positive link.

I spent an entire day washing and tooling around the bike. Packing and unpacking for the most effective and logical way of retrieving stuff from the rucksack. I had a problem tying the rucksack to the bike. It was a half-hour job every morning and I would soon learn that at times it needed retying during the day too.

The owner of the resort was a jovial character called Rajen, a walking jewellery shop. Balding and fat, a producer of Malayalam movies who also had business interests in Dubai, he dazzled everyone with the gold and diamonds on his person, and bemused you with his confident, ungrammatical English. 'Where you are now?' he asked me. 'Here,' I replied. 'No, I mean, "Where you going next?".' 'There,' I said, pointing in the general direction of the north. And a hearty cheer resounded to this piece of intellectual give-and-take. Rajen is great company over a bottle of Scotch. His Scotch.

Next stop was with a one-time colleague of mine in the government-controlled milk business in the early 1990s. Mr Thomas was a senior manager of the milk union in the Malabar region when I was posted there as managing director of the same institution. He taught me the basics of business management and I am forever grateful to him. The ride to his house in Kochi, the commercial capital of Kerala, took four hours. Mr Thomas had a penchant for wiping away tears while talking about the injustices heaped on him by the government during his official career. Now, he runs his own, successful traditional *peda* sweets business.

This was my first really long motorcycle ride on the national highways of Kerala. I had travelled extensively by road, but always in the comfort of a chauffeur-driven car. The number of accidents on Kerala's roads is one of the highest per capita in India. The obvious reasons are narrow roads, habitation throughout the road length, too many vehicles, over-speeding and drunken driving. Over-speeding is the crux of the matter, and here the typical Malayali ego trip comes into play: *I can drive faster and better than any fucker on the road.* And then, BAM! So with one eye on the rearview mirror, and hugging the side of the road, I puttered into Kochi.

Before I took leave of my host and headed off for

Palghat, I left a cheque for two lakh rupees with Mr Thomas to help him tide over his expansion programmes. To be returned over the next few months. He never asked me for the loan. It was an offer from my side. This was the point of the journey. Pay off as many of the karmic debts as possible. However small they may be. Sometimes, as small as exchanging a smile.

The traffic eases as I reach the district of Palghat. I see a man pee on the side of the road. This is the rarest of rare sights in Kerala because of the density of the population—and the general absence of the penile exhibitionism rampant elsewhere in the country. I stop the bike and pee in joyful brotherhood with him.

Kandath Tharavad is owned by Bhagwal Das in Thenkurussi village in the Palghat district of Kerala. It is a classy village resort, offering only a few rooms. Bhagwal Das has sad eyes and is from an old moneyed family of the area. The family fortunes saw its ups and downs. After working abroad he has finally settled down to running this resort. His constant companion is a fellow called Reghu whose pastime appears to be leering at village belles bathing in the village tank.

I had been getting some press locally, and Kerala has more than its share of offbeat people curious to know more about one. Krishnadas, I figured, was a kook, and had wanted to meet me for more than a month. He found out that I was in his hometown and came to meet me with his wife in tow. It turned out that he was a young information technology professional with his head screwed on straight. He was merely fascinated with my meanderings on a mobike. He rang me up regularly, all through the nine months I was on the road. Talk about connections in life! Made easier now, of course, courtesy the mobile.

Bhaskar Panicker's services are for hire in this resort. He is an astrologer, and Bhagwal swears by him. I consulted him, and he said money would 'flow' after a certain date. He didn't say in which direction. If nothing else, these guys are great showmen. Two sweet old Aussie ladies were brought to the resort by Pradeep 'Cools', a guide from Bangalore. Cools was a non-stop talker and I kind of liked him. Had good music, my kind of music in his mobile. The ladies provided my first close-up with people from down under. I was charmed.

The Gandhi Foundation guys came to see me. This was a new one. Their take on the subject was that I was doing a Herculean job for national integration. Despite the absurdity I solemnly agreed with their astute observation. You don't argue with holy cows. Gandhi and national integration—it doesn't get holier than that.

What's with me and national integration? The notion

seems to follow me around everywhere. It occurred to me that even being sent to Kerala to work was part of the national integration policy. Was it because I am from the merged state of Sikkim and needed to be reminded constantly of my loyalty to India? Had some spook agency been tailing me and felt the need to set the record straight? Some things follow you to your grave, I guess.

4

Saying goodbye to a part of your life is a little painful even if you are a cold fish. That reminds me. Food. Food in Kerala is to die for. Fish, chicken, pork, beef, whatever, all cooked in delectable coconut oil. Except *putte*—a rice-based cylindrical piece of poison which can choke you during breakfast. I suspect this dish was created to get rid of guests who overstay. Have I stumbled on one of Kerala's darkest secrets? Kuttapan, the 'in-law' specialist, claims to love *putte* and serves it diligently to his mom-in-law when she is on one of her infrequent visits.

Bhagwal and his friends, along with a local TV crew, saw me off at the border with Tamil Nadu. Tiripur is a textile town. Tim Heinemann does his bit to add to India's burgeoning export of manufactured garments. Born of missionary parents, Tim became a naturalized Indian in 1972. He loves India. I first met him when he was selling garments at Kovalam beach way back in 1986. He also happened to train the first batch of lifeguards at that beach—on the sole basis of a single manual he'd picked up on the subject.

Tim picked me up from near the railway station. Blue eyes and a quick smile. We had lunch at a Tamil dhaba. His home is a rented house almost out of town. A daughter from one of his marriages stays with him now. A chequered life about sums his up. Hippie, farmer, beach bum, entrepreneur. Been there, bought the teeshirt. We slept on his rooftop after he had sniffed the speed and direction of the wind that night. Like a general, he organized our defences against the huge mosquitoes by burning repellent tablets. These had to be placed at exactly the right height and direction to get maximum coverage over the thin mattresses on the rooftop. We slept after a beer and a dinner of twelve eggs and two loaves of brown bread between us. Talk about American excesses, even though he is a naturalized Indian. Childhood habits, I guess. There were no fans working inside Tim's house, so the rooftop was a natural setting on that hot March night.

Tim speaks Tamil fluently and he translated a vociferous argument between the labourers and the owner of a house being newly constructed nearby. In Sikkim a few decades ago, carpenters and labourers were treated as royalty when a house was being built. Millet beer, foaming in bamboo containers, would be held out worshipfully by the owners. This amazing tradition had its roots in the belief that there should be no negative vibrations when building a house. This is all but lost now. I imagine Tim's neighbour is happy enough in his new house.

Tiripur to Madurai took seven hours. The longest ride so far. Numbness all the way below the waist. I cowboy-walk into a rundown hotel. The first in a long series. Quick bath and a long sleep.

Jesudasan Rajasekaran. Servant of Jesus Rajasekaran. Freak Rajasekaran, in my opinion. Fifty-eight years old, with boundless energy. I get tired seeing him just bounce around a room. Short, balding and spectacled. He looks like a professor and does not behave like one. Went to Bangalore to buy his first guitar in his teens and got his cock sucked on the return night bus by an old fogey. All the while clutching his guitar. The rock star of the swinging 1970s in south India. Electric Vethalapah, Temple Tramps, Bluebirds and Yannamalai International are some of the bands that he sang with in Madurai and elsewhere. Still strums a mean guitar and smokes dope with gusto. Had the honour of a pipe with him. Just plain crazy.

What do you do with a dinosaur that refuses to die? You go to Dindigul to visit the eunuchs with him. Dindigul is a couple of hours away. We went roaring there on my bike with Rajasekaran driving and yelling 'Whoa-a-a' all the way. On the back of a motorcycle, age catches up. Next guy I want to share a ride with is Mick Jagger.

I have never been comfortable with the eunuch community and this was a chance to bond. Theirs is a close-knit group. Rajasekaran waded in among his old friends. Squeezing an arm here, a torso there. Introductions over, Nandini the eunuch took charge, and this is what I learnt about the gay community. The Panthis are at the bottom (literally) of the hierarchy. They only thrust. While the Kothis only receive. The double-deckers do both. Bisexuals come next. Followed by the Satla Kothis who are cross-dressers and have sex with men. At the top of the heap are the Aravanis, or eunuchs, who have been operated upon. I hung around with them for a few hours and they have stories—like we do, only different. We who-a-a-ed our way back to Madurai.

Serviced the bike. It gleamed and looked ready to rock. Oops! Sorry! Ready to roll. That was the Electric Vethalapah effect. Tamils are extremely courteous. Everybody is a Sir. A young woman on a scooter told me that my side-stand was up. The only unknown woman to engage with me on her own initiative throughout the journey—if you discount the obscene gesture made to me by a prostitute somewhere in north India. The ride to Karaikkudi, the home of the Chettiar community, took around three hours. Easy, sedate riding. Hot, hot, hot. Riding in this weather in south India was a mistake. Have to drink at least three litres of water to stay ahead of the game.

Karaikkudi and me. We know each other. A few months ago I had come to this place to do a small cameo in a Tamil movie called *Periyar*, after the legendary Tamil politician. The role was insignificant but I loved it, hamming it up like hell. Unfortunately, the day I was shooting there were no actresses around. My shit luck. It's another thing that had they been there, I would have only ogled them from a safe distance. Bureaucracy emasculates you. And shit luck follows emasculation.

This time I was here to meet the dowager Mrs Meyappan at her resort, 'The Bungalow'. Forceful personality. Old but frightfully active. Lovely resort. Great food. She oversees the serving of food to her patrons personally. One feels the wind of the great past in her presence. She sent me with a guide to visit some of the great Chettiar mansions. Gargantuan houses stretching from street to street filled with Belgian glass, Swedish enamel, Italian marble, tiles from Britain and teak from Burma. The rooms are small and without furniture. Massive courtyards inside the house. Most are verging on dilapidation. Ornate and ostentatious. Karaikkudi and me. We know each other better now.

Karaikkudi to Nagaipatinam to Pondicherry. Twelve hours straight. What do I remember? Excruciating pain in the posterior. Welts whiplashed on the sexy butt.

Masochistic? You bet! To top it all I couldn't find a hotel in a hurry. Finally, down by the beach, a sad-looking receptionist gave me a room in an ashram. Before handing over the keys he read out the riot act to me. No smoking, no drinking, no female company, etc. etc. Yeah, yeah, I felt like asking him if it was okay to masturbate, since he was silent on the subject. I went into the room and promptly lit up. Got a pint later and guzzled it. If I did anything else by myself, I'm not telling.

5

Skedaddled from the place. To Chennai. Presidency Club, where the rich frolic. Nice, clean room. Renjith Jacob was the host. He is into business and has a lovely circle of friends, like Raghavram and Joseph. They took me into their fold and it was party time. Five-star parties and the best booze available. Raghavram took me for breakfast at Woodlands, a drive-in restaurant where they clamp trays of southern food on your car windows. Those trays fascinated me. Crows were being fed by many people in memory of their ancestors.

Raghavram took me to meet Harold Rose, a Tai Chi instructor. We arranged for an intensive ten-day course. Tai Chi has always fascinated me. Images of the ancient Chinese swirling to a soundless tune had reached into my depths. Looks easier than it is. Much easier. The system is very hard on the hips and the balance required is phenomenal. Harold was very patient with me and I thank him for the courtesies extended. Initially, I'd planned to stay only for a couple of days in Chennai, but my resolve to do as I pleased came into play.

Dr Elangovan, once a colleague of mine, made alternative arrangements for me to stay. I don't know how many dinners I filched off him and his wonderful wife. Dr Elangovan is the only man to have climbed on to my back with his knee on my spine. He is a medical doctor by training and a decade ago, when I complained of back pain, he employed that tactic. I am free of the pain now. I suspect the good doctor frightened it away. A thick, black, hairy knee is a formidable weapon, believe me.

The director of the Tamil movie I acted in, Rajashekaran, was in Chennai too. He has won a number of national and state awards, and is also a playwright and novelist. I simply can't figure what he's doing in the bureaucracy. We bond because we stand as co-contemners of the Supreme Court in a case lodged involving a department of which we had both been Secretaries at different points of time. He gave me the role in a moment of weakness just before we entered the Supreme Court. He may have regretted it but I don't and I remain forever grateful to him. However, the expected deluge of roles from the Tamil film industry never came my way. Another bridge burnt, and we moved on.

The Tai Chi classes went on in full swing, as did the social gigs. Joseph gave me a specially made Harley jacket from his own export unit, and a book by Paulo Coelho. I sang at a karaoke party and jammed up with a drummer in another house. Harold looked more desperate by the day but I kept trying. Decades in the government had taken their toll. I cannot swing to the rhythm of nature, I cannot focus and push my energy around. I'm too used to being pushed around myself. Time will heal this imbalance. In the meantime Harold suffered. And so did I.

Chennai was a blast but it was time to go. The summer heat finally got to me and I decided to head for the Himalayas. The change of plans was to occur frequently during the journey. I was supposed to travel around south India and gradually work my way up north, but ended up zigzagging around the country.

Chennai to Vijayawada was a blistering nine hours. Royal roger of a road. I'd replaced the jeans I'd worn earlier with baggy cotton pants. Jockeys, I found, were the best undergarments, because even a minor crease around the posterior can play havoc after a few hours. At times I've had to raise myself from the bike to give air and solace to the weeping twins.

Lunch on the wayside involved the attentions of a gaping cook and waiter. Who says we are not one nation? We have many common characteristics. Gaping, for one.

Since it was getting dark in Vijayawada, I asked a cop to suggest a decent hotel to put up at. I obviously looked like Ratan Tata's relative because he sent me to a bloody expensive place. Since I was now a Tai Chi cat, I decided to splurge for a night.

Vijayawada to Visakhapatnam was eight hours. I don't

remember much of that ride because I was numb from the shock of the night's charges. The exuberance of a slightly tipsy evening quickly deteriorates to chills in the early morning, when you're presented with a bill that only Bill Gates would regard with equanimity. I am not a miser. Never was, never will be. But a government pensioner hasn't a lot to go on.

Look at me. I worked for exactly twenty years. I never saved any earned leave because I was dislocated socially and had to take long leave when visiting home (if I'd forgone leave, I would have saved money). Then, even after commutation of pension, that is, taking 40 per cent of my pension for the next fifteen years in advance, I got a total of twelve lakh. I had to pay back eight lakh which I had taken as a loan to build a house. Cash in hand: four lakh. The sum a young management professional takes home in a month. And which had to last me for a year.

Today, somewhere between Vijayawada and Visakhapatnam, I had black stuff coming out of my eyes. It was all that dust and the exhaust fumes, my constant companions on the road. Despite the goggles and the eye-drops, this problem was going to stay with me. Another red-letter moment was crap time on the side of the road. People saw my ass, whiplashes and all. The kick-start was sticking and the self-starter had developed a mind of its own. Just one of those days. The silver lining was that a roadside mechanic fixed the kick-start and would not hear of taking any money. And the food at the end of the day in Visakhapatnam was exquisite.

Visakhapatnam to Bhubaneswar, the capital of Orissa, takes around ten hours. Given the distance, further updates on my health would be meaningless. The four-lane road in Andhra Pradesh continued into Orissa. I found that the traffic had eased. No, the traffic had stopped completely. But it was a spanking new road and I whistled a gay tune to keep my spirits up. Freedom!

In a ditch. The bloody road just finished off in a ditch. Under construction, I guessed. I had missed the diversion completely. Resolved to keep my eyes open in the future and my mind on the road. No damage was done, as I landed right side up.

By then, I had built up a sort of a comfortable rhythm on the road. There were the mandatory five-minute piss/ cigarette stops after every one-and-a-half to two hours. Drank water while driving and stopped for around half an hour each for breakfast and lunch. Without realizing it, I had developed a habit of vigorously rubbing my behind as soon as I got off the bike. It felt like the correct thing to do. Then I would get down on my haunches to smoke while methodically going over the luggage and the bike. That's evolution for you. During the ass-rubbing part I would survey my immediate surroundings for potential troublemakers. I had had to scoot after the survey a couple of times.

But there was a general sense of comfort, actually. Somewhere on that stretch of road I'd crossed the threshold as a biker. I'd become a biker. *Lord, I'd become a biker!* I knew it. Like all seminal experiences, the feeling is not possible to describe in full. There is a subtle shift at the way you look at your bike. Feel it, actually. It was almost sexual. Every moment you know what your comfort speed should be. The thud-thud of the bike tells you a story. The subtle change of vibrations warns you. I still know nothing about the mechanics of the bike but I know the bike. Follow me? If not, try it out for yourself. You won't be disappointed.

Thakur, my old, old buddy, was waiting for me at Bhubaneswar. Cheshire smile and a Cro-Magnon skull. Thinks he has killer looks. Out popped a bottle and we hit it mercilessly. Then I was forced to listen to old Himachali songs. And more Himachali songs. G.V.V. Sharma, another old pal, walked in to rescue me. The last time I had seen him, he'd been a teetotaller; now he can guzzle with the best. Some changes are for the better.

Orissa being one of the backward states, I was curious to know about the lives of the tribals there. Sharma promised to arrange for my stay in Mayurbhanj district. We went for lunch to the Bhubaneswar Club. Nice. Met some local journalists. Got plunked on a website. Thakur promised to find me a cottage in Manali, his hometown. The place where we were staying was some government corporation guest house. The cook was amazing, but so were we.

6

Mayurbhanj district. Malaria-prone. Met Vineel Krishna, IAS under training. Flashback to P.G. Tenzing, IAS under training, Kasargod district, Kerala. What does a jaded ex tell a bright-eyed officer? Nothing. You listen to him and hear yourself a couple of decades ago. The circle of life goes on. You graciously let it go. The same reasons for joining the government: serving the country, the poor, making a difference, going to places and postings, etc.

The government services are generally reviled by the chattering classes and, at times, rightly so. However, in defence of the services, I have to say that many officers work hard and honestly under extremely adverse conditions and still make a difference in the lives of some of the poor of our land. That is the gospel truth. I swear I have seen saints at work who could make you feel worthless. On the flipside, there are also those ghouls who enter into a macabre dance with pot-bellied netas. All on high moral ground. Made me think, this meeting with the young officer in a rural setting. Sigh! He is right and so am I. He for joining and I for leaving.

You never really get over the culture shock of alien surroundings, especially if you are urbanized and Westernized. When you don't know the language or the etiquette. The thought processes and the politics. Most of my time in Kerala went in a haze of semi-understanding, despite my learning the language. The undercurrents remain un-understood. The subtle jokes missed. The caste and religious factors baffle you. There is no family or social support. You are operating at thirty per cent capacity and you know it. I was sent to Kasargod, where Malayalam, Kannada and Tulu are spoken. I did not even know Malayalam then. What does that say about the system? Or the logic that drives it?

I remember my days as a trainee. Loafing around from room to room occupied by bored old farts who were dying for you to leave. Trying to look interested in and enthusiastic about statistics. Lying through my teeth to the district collector, my local deity. Feeling horny, lonely and out of place. Rummaging through the district library for a book in English, any book in English. Listening to the faithful walkman. Grateful Dead, Kris Kristofferson, The Who, Pink Floyd, J.J. Cale, and all. Watching Asthana, the Indian Police Service officer, train his empty gun on the quivering waiter. Waiting desperately for a letter from my girlfriend, who later became my wife. Running away at any excuse to anywhere else. Trying desperately to look official and busy. Giving cocky ones to the politicians. Wondering what the fuck I was doing there. Eating 'peas-fry' and *borottas*, the Kerala roti, over and over again.

One day, the then Communist chief minister, E.K. Nayanar, was putting up at the district rest house and I went to call on him. He was in a torn vest and smoking a beedi. This furthered the dreamlike quality of my training. Comrade Nayanar turned out to be one of the best-loved and successful politicians of Kerala.

Bapi, an official of the NGO (non-governmental organization) called Sambandh, took me to Bhalupani, near a town called Jassipur in Orissa. I was to live in a village with the Santhal and Kolha tribes. I was given a traditional welcome with flowers, which embarrassed me. I stayed in the house of Basanti, the president of an organization doing social work.

While walking around the village, I was offered, in some houses, a potent and viscous fluid called russi, a rice beer widely consumed in the area. Had to drink the stuff as a matter of courtesy. One old bandicoot found relish in torturing me by never letting the glass go empty. There is not enough to eat in these parts. The staple diet is mostly watery rice with salt. A special occasion is marked with a feast of boiled edible leaves from the forest along with raw onion and chilly. Most of the work is done by women, while the men drink the blues away. Some forage in the forest for firewood and minor forest produce to sell in the daily market. Medicine depends on the shaman or a couple of private clinics. People here are convinced that no cure is ever complete without an injection. So every visit to the quack is accompanied by a shot. I wonder what the syringes contain.

The strange thing about this village is the cleanliness. No garbage. They have nothing to buy from the markets, so there is no refuse. There are no cats and dogs in the village, because there is no food for them. They would be competition, in fact, for a source of protein: field mice. This is a part of India we rarely see or hear about. There are millions of such people without hope. I sense a great betrayal from our side.

Basanti is thirty-six years old. Studied up to class seven. Steady eyes, quiet resolve, flashes of humour, a no-nonsense attitude; no wonder she never married. She had tried to fight the local self-government elections and had been defeated by groups with vested interests. I was happy to see that despite the overall social milieu, there are people like Basanti who never give up. Her self-help group engages in honey-processing, and the making of soap and *siali* leaf plates and similar items, and has a turnover of more than five lakh a year. A huge sum in that area.

Then there are people like Bapi, educated, dedicated, satisfied with their personal lot, committed to the tribes, acting as a catalyst for change, spending decades in the boondocks, true champions.

The children followed me everywhere. Even peeking into my room through the windows. They brought me a local fruit to eat. I took some pictures and showed them in the digital camera. The whoops of joy were ear-shattering. On the last night the entire village came to see me. Who are you, why are you here, will you get us electricity; will you get us drinking water, a road? Then the rhythmic thump of the drums and the dancing, self joining in. One woman told me that she would have invited me to her house but she had nothing to offer a guest. Made me want to cry.

An enduring image of my visit to Bhalupani was that of an old lady leaning on a walking stick, carrying water to her hut from a well. Back and forth. Again and again. She had no relatives and survived on handouts from the villagers. I really do not know why I went to meet the people of Bhalupani. Just another turn on the road, I guess, so I could bring their story to you.

Simlipal Tiger Reserve is a few hours away from Bhalupani. I drove the bike cautiously through the jungle, keeping a wary eye out for its wilder denizens. The forest guest house is basic and if you bring the provisions the chaps there cook them. Some tribal boys from a neighbouring village had heard the bike and came to eye the machine and the man. Then there was this forest contractor with a whore. I am sure she was a whore. Bright-red lipstick and powdered face. The contractor sped off after finding me at the guest house. All was quiet after that. Took solitary walks in the forest. Two days of looking inward. Then back to Mayurbhanj for the night.

I got a call from Kerala saying that the Supreme Court wanted to see my mug on a particular date that month. On the same contempt case in the course of which Rajashekaran capitulated and gave me a role in his Tamil film he had been denying me for a decade. This again called for a change of plans. I zipped across to Kolkata, the nearest metro to Mayurbhanj, in order to resume my journey home to Sikkim, to catch a few days there before I stood before the awful majesty of the law.

Subrat, the optimist, had given me a place to stay in Kolkata. The guy is a product of the Indian Institutes of Technology as well as Management. A double whammy. What he is doing pushing files is beyond my comprehension. He likes to discuss Buddhism and life's eternal mysteries with me. I usually give him a lot of made-up claptrap. These brainy types normally fall for it. This time I gave him *The Tibetan Book of the Dead* to read. That should give him food for some thought. I spent a day browsing through malls and seeing two movies back to back. I do that once in a while. When I find time I go to a multiplex and soak in a couple of films. The security people give me funny looks and a more thorough check the second time I enter. Sometimes, by the third entrance, we are on nodding terms. Kolkata is a crazy place. Its premier football clubs have different fish as mascots, and the price of these in the market shoots up or falls with a thud depending on which team is the winner of the match on a given day.

It was a twelve-hour ride to Raigunj, on my way to Sikkim. I ran over a snake today. I saw another that had come under someone's wheels, whirling in its death throes. Saw a third on the side of the road. Didn't know what it meant. I kept repeating prayers for the snakes. I drove slowly, feeling a little creepy. Rest for the night was in another forgettable hotel on the roadside. Nearing home now.

Siliguri was just five hours away. Made it in good time and met Yogdeep Gurung, an old psychotic friend. He had hit his blind roommate with a wooden stool for stealing his weed when we were in college. Another time I'd fixed him up with a date, and just after the introductions were over, he proceeded to puke wholeheartedly on the table. Was already blind drunk before the date. That's Yogi for you. He is also a stand-up guy and many were the times we slugged it out shoulder to shoulder against the villains of Delhi. We have puked together in the communal puke bucket after a session of brown sugar. He is now a pillar of the community in which he lives. We were planning to do some business. He and me. Hah!

7

The ride to Gangtok was smooth. Just as I was savouring the achievement of this cross-country ride, I was stopped at a point an hour from home. An officious-looking team from the transport and police departments had set up shop in the middle of the highway and was ostensibly checking papers. I am, by-and-large, a law-abiding sort of chap and so I handed the documents to the cop who stopped me. He told me to carry them myself over to the prick behind the makeshift desk. 'Like hell,' I roared. 'The fuck can come across and see them if he wants.' There was a long line of vehicles on both sides of the road and I had parked in the middle of the highway. I shamelessly played to the gallery. 'Corrupt assholes! Want to make money, huh?' Someone in my audience tittered. After that, the bloody creeps literally begged me to go away. Suddenly, nobody wanted to check my ID. I was OK. I roared off in disdain, enjoying my little victory over petty officialdom immensely.

My small triumph over institutionalized corruption.

This is the land of my birth. Hopefully, I will die here. I could never really live here, though. Schooling was mostly outside the state, as a boarder. College in Delhi. Job at the age of twenty-two in Kerala. I did come home for a few years between, though, and worked on deputation in the state and central governments. But that was only for short stints.

To make up for lost time, I gazed my fill at Kanchendzonga, the mighty mountain that is also our guardian deity. I've loved it since childhood. It speaks to me. People who don't have this bond with any part of this living planet are sadly missing out on something. Pang Lhabsol is observed in Sikkim every year. This is a festival where prayers are offered to Kanchendzonga for the protection it offers us.

Menda, my elder daughter, had cooked a lovely welcoming meal. She is turning out to be a fine young woman, no thanks to me. All credit for bringing up the children goes to my long-suffering wife. We have lived apart for the better part of our married life because we've both held government jobs in different parts of the country. She has raised the children as a single mother. Cheers to matriarchy. I regret the fact of not being there for the children, but there was nothing much I could do about it now. Hope they turn out to be stable like their mother. Two daughters for a male chauvinist pig. I was a hardcore pig till my college days. Then came the first girl and then another. Till I woke up one fine day, a feminist to the core. I love it when nature teaches you a lesson you'll never forget. It makes you a better human being. My mother-in-law lives with my wife and daughters. I got her as part of the dowry. Now my family has six women, including two women servants. Thus, the pig is alone.

So, onto a flight to Delhi, to obey the court summons. This was a convoluted case, a typical example of the state government getting it all wrong. The net result was an enraged Supreme Court looking down two loaded barrels at us quavering babus. Four Secretaries who were the department-in-charge at different points of time were hauled up on the charge of contempt of court. This was the second time I was standing in the court for the same charge. The justices looked awesome in their majesty. What power they wield! (*'Hang them. Send these culprits in for a day. Or just let them go . . . Next case.'*) The rush in the courtroom was unbelievable. The top lawyers rushed from bench to bench. Gowns flying, juniors trailing, clients about to cry.

Pandemonium. Something was brought about by the state government and the Bench was pleased to note it and dispense with our presence for the near future. Whew! Joy prompted us to skip down the court's steps.

I went with my friend of the Cro-Magnon skull to search for a house in Manali. Those two or three days—don't really remember exactly how many—were spent in a haze of boozy exuberance. Guys like Khan, Pampu, Beniram, Vijay, Basha and Vipin were coming and going all day. We were also coming and going in and out of our senses, but drinking all the way. That was the time I found myself feeding momos to Beniram from my plate, and wondering why.

Found a nice cottage where I was to write my magnum opus. Thakur took me to meet his relatives and they were Cro-Magnons all. Wow! Felt like the old times. Grunting while dancing, feasting with abandon, casting all table etiquette to the winds, tearing the meat off the bones with my hands and—on at least one occasion—my feet.

Back to Sikkim to boast about my narrow escape from the law. I took the bike to Mangan, in north Sikkim, our ancestral home. I have relatives there. And friends. The Eros of Mangan for instance. The guy has spent his life in the pursuit of sex and the conclusions he's drawn from his experiences. He is convinced about the correctness of his generalizations. If I told you all his theories, I'd be risking offending some of you, so I'll confine myself to just a few: having sex with your wife daily ensures her fidelity to you; the act of sex is the best exercise because every part of the body is involved (including yanking at your partner's hair, which constitutes a scalp massage); the trick to finding out if a woman is faking an orgasm is to look for a faint flush on her chest; women are horniest after eleven in the night; the way to delay ejaculation is to press the depression between the asshole and the balls. This is what we talked about in Mangan. Intellectually stimulating stuff. Stimulating otherwise, too.

Mangan is a small town. Population less than 5,000. Everybody knows everybody else and what they do all day. What they ate for breakfast and what time they shat. That sort of town. One of my good friends, Jigmi, is the town marshal. He starts his day early. By 6 a.m. he has started his rounds. He criss-crosses the town, drinking copious amounts of tea. Sometimes, he even wakes up couples in their bedrooms. By 9 a.m. he is back at home, satisfied that all is well in his town.

Then there is my cousin who is a seismologist trained in the USA. He wound up back in his hometown growing cardamom. He uses old socks as gloves while working in the cardamom fields. Pemzang is the first completely asexual man I have met. Hardcore bachelor. Not gay. Nothing. No known girlfriends or boyfriends. Mangan knows. Mangan cares. Mangan can't figure out this eccentric. His passion at this juncture is to oppose the environmentally damaging mega hydel projects thrust on this land and these people. Fascinating character.

Met my father's elder brother, and his wife, who loves me dearly, and Dad's elder sister. Mangan has more than its share of freaks for such a small town. I spent my childhood years in this town when an offer of a samosa or a jalebi was the ultimate treat. Where riding goats, bulls and mules was a part of life. Where scratched elbows and knees barely got a second look in the house. Where the kitchen and the toilet were always separate from the main house. Where pissing in the night was an opportunity to try and see your dad's pecker. Where bullying my younger brother gave me hours of pleasure. Where stealing the neighbour's fruits was the expected thing to do. Where watching the Indian army convoys from the hilltop was a must-see. Where getting whacked on the butt by a cane wielded by my father was a regular affair. Where getting to know my first English alphabet was from Anthony, a Malayali. My destination was clear from those days, only I did not know it at the time.

8

As I write this, I get the news that a young cousin that I was fond of has died, leaving behind a young wife and a daughter. Saddening and maddening. Chewang Pazo, you unlucky unfortunate. You with a broken karma. Scored with misery. No even breaks in life. Orphaned early. Leaving behind a widow and a child you will never watch grow up. Repeating the tragedy of your parents. Goodbye, brother.

Death. My favourite topic. Been wondering about death ever since my hormones started jangling. Why? When? Where? There was a time when I used to cower with fear thinking about my final moment. Now, after a few brushes with the event, I find myself pretty calm about it. Maybe the only real progress I have made in life. I am beginning to grasp the theory of impermanence. The holy detachment to everything, including one's life.

My first experience of death, up close and personal at

the age of thirty-four was when my father died. I was holding him and shouting at him not to give up. My mother gently told me to let him go and started reciting prayers in his ear. Her pillar in this life was dying and she let him go with dignity. An unforgettable lesson. Transporting him back home in the ambulance was a blur except for the headache of a lifetime. A Buddhist funeral in Sikkim is one messy and long affair. The mourning period is a full forty-nine days. In between, we had to take Dad's ashes to Bodhgaya—Mom, Dad's younger sister and me. This was my first visit to the holiest place for Buddhists. I felt a blast of energy pass through me inside the main temple. I have never been the same since. Don't ask me what happened that day. I don't know, except that it was Dad's parting gift to me. I really loved my old man.

Then came my own fight. Millennium night. The whole world was celebrating, but not this family. I was told that I had lung cancer. ('*Six months at the most.*') The diagnosis was wrong; it was hepatitis C. That gave me a longer period to survive but medicines were then at the trial stage, with a 30-per-cent chance of success. I took injections, initially daily, then spaced out over days, for two years. The family stood firmly by my side. Meditation and faith were a big, big help. I used to talk to my cells too.

His Holiness, the Dodrupchen Rimpoche, and His Eminence, the Lachen Rimpoche, gave me their blessings and prayed for me. There was tremendous support from family and friends. This was a long face-off with the ultimate winner. I walked the hospitals of Delhi. Searching for the right doctor, till I found him. Dr Sarin, a disciple of Sai Baba, pulled me through. God bless him. These extra years I got are his.

I used to observe the patients waiting their turn in the queue. That is the time you see the hopelessness, the utter despair of being poor. No money for medicines. No money to live. I will never forget that. I will never forget.

The other time was my fault. It happened on the road from Mangan to Gangtok, around 9.30 at night. I was driving a four-wheel SUV at high speed with a few beers inside me on a steep mountain road—a recipe for disaster. Disaster did not disappoint. I fell thirty feet with the vehicle to the road down below. Luck! It could have been curtains. The split second I took to land went both in slow motion and quick as a flash. I was calm. All the years of meditation had paid off. No panic. No fear. No regrets. It is my understanding that the last state of mind in this life determines the next. So, to train for death is to cultivate equanimity. Looks like I'm getting there.

If you believe in rebirth, it seems to make sense. The law of nature is very clear. So you sow, so shall you reap. You can't plant an orange pip and expect an apple tree to grow from it. You can't die with a terrified mind and expect a calm, new next life.

I'd broken most of the bones on the left of my upper body. Collar-bone and six ribs. People arrived and took me to the local hospital. Then followed a few months of rest and recreation. The bloody bones still ache when it's cold. A burden for life. I asked for it. The darkly funny upshot was that the turning where the accident took place is now known as the 'P.G. Turning'.

Twice, at close quarters, makes a body think. Makes the sorting of priorities kind of easy. The first time, I sorted out some of my wrinkles. The second time was a clear clarion call to do my stuff before it was too late. The insanity of my life appalled me. With a vengeance, I got to work. Chucked up my job, which did not interest me anymore. On the quiet I had built up a hotel chain (all leased) as a post-retirement career. But now I knew life was too short. I wanted to do a ride on a motorcycle, and when better than now? The idea of writing a book came up when I was with Dicky, my cousin, her husband Ramesh and some of their friends in journalism. The idea was quickly relayed by the *Telegraph*'s Bishakha De Sarkar to Prita Maitra in Penguin Books, who led me by the hand, kicking and screaming though I was, into what was for me a new world: publishing. One thing led to another and I ended up signing a contract with Penguin to write about my travels.

Death is an aspect of life that is not popularly discussed. It's like a dirty secret everyone shares. Most cultures do not encourage talking about it. My father tried to prepare us for death. He used to talk about its certainty, its inevitability.

So when I started my search for life's meaning, death was a significant part of the equation. I am nowhere near understanding anything, but am at this point comfortable with the idea of death. It happens. Shit happens. Be prepared. Prepare your family, friends and all who will listen. Morbid? No way! This is the way of the wise. Read any religious text. Life is after all a journey to death and the next life. Lord Buddha's first words after gaining enlightenment were: '*Countless lives have I lived.*' The man had no reason to lie. I believe in him.

9

Off to Nepal, only a few hours from Sikkim. Hopped on to the old bike. We were a team now. On a sub-continental ride together. I have a story about the gear I carried around. It has to do with Karchoong, he of the extraordinary talent and the big, round head. Cartoonist, writer, lensman and computer whiz-kid, who is also an Enfield freak. We met and he had the gear, and he gave. Saddlebags and a bag with magnets for the tank, and a net for the carrier bag. Two minutes flat to load all of it. He saved me a lot of grief on the road after that. Bless his big heart. And his big head.

A twelve-hour ride to Birganj, where my maternal uncle stays. Met my cousin Sonam, who was on his way home from Kathmandu, at a point near Birganj. The highlight of this ride was the first serious rainfest. Respect the rain, my man, or suffer. Was not really prepared to tackle the elements. I am learning. Quickly. I stopped to have lunch at Itahari and was offered much more than lunch. This must have been a whore joint where only garishly painted waitresses served inedible food and asked if they could serve anything more. I should have realized. Indifferent food and a chatty, painted waitress should have warned me. The pat on the head was the final straw, and I bolted.

My uncle is a self-made man and he drinks whisky that's just about okay. I got on his back for that. Now, at least when I'm around, he drinks Scotch. He deserves it. Started out with nothing and made it big. These rags-to-riches guys are special. Hats off to this breed all over the world. He is still handsome and careful with his appearance. Turns a few heads even now, the old dog. Stayed a couple of days at Birganj. Shithole of a place. It's neither India nor Nepal, although officially in the second.

Sonam regaled me with his life's antics. Small-time mafia instincts. Thank God he is on the straight and the narrow now. My aunt has such an elaborate prayer ceremony to a pantheon of gods that she could have taught a temple full of priests the ropes. No wonder Uncle is still handsome and agile.

Went to Kathmandu the Palung way. Seven thousand feet. Rain, rain and more rain. Slow ride, with fog for company. Hungry and cold. I found myself trying to warm my hands in the glow of a cigarette. Funny, but true. Needed to pee and had to search for the thing. Ye gods! A drenched organ is a non-existent one.

Kathmandu, here I come. Joey, here I come. Joey is

an enigma. Joey lives near Boudha, a holy place. It has not changed Joey. It's Boudha I'm worried about—it's had Joey living there for some years now. Joey is successful in his chosen career. He parties regularly with the Page-Three crowd of Kathmandu. He plays golf with the rich, successful, bold and the beautiful. He has a succession of gorgeous women on his arms on different social occasions. He looks successful and happy.

Joey has a secret sorrow. He does not have a steady girlfriend and has to work hard to maintain his sex life on an even keel. He blurted out his dilemma during a mellow evening. An evening for sharing secrets. I had some dope presented to me in Manali. Since I am normally an abstemious man, it had stayed with me. Joey lunged for it with a fanatical gleam in his eyes. He does not smoke either, so I asked who the end-user was. Then he spilled the beans. Joey takes his women seriously. This piece of dope was for a lady on the rebound who would be reaching Kathmandu after a month. In Joey's own words, 'I thrive on rebounding women.'

One of this man's modus operandi is what I call the 'kitchen cuddle'. This is when Joey invites a prospective lay for lunch or dinner. The wine is uncorked and the servants are thrown out. Then he weaves his magic in the kitchen, apron and all. Exotic spices, unusual condiments and elaborate rituals are part of the atmosphere. He claims that the more complicated the cooking, the better his chances of success. All the time the wine glasses are kept topped up, and scintillating conversation ensues. (Something about a man in a kitchen enhances his sex appeal, according to an expert.) Then Joey gets happy.

We have a ritual whenever I go to Kathmandu. We storm the casinos at once. Sometimes as many as three different ones in a night. All to lose money. Casinos are for suckers and I'm a big one. These places have a lot of characters with hard-luck stories who pluck at your sleeve and whine in your ear in the hope of a few bucks. Bright, garish, bad performers, unsavoury characters and bouncers. Wonder why I go there.

This time, for once, I went sightseeing, with my cousin Deki Piya and her hubby Dijan, a major in the army. To Nagarkot. Kathmandu and its surrounding hills are visually stunning. The Thakali food is simply delicious and also wholesome. The stupid car stalled. We pushed and prayed. It worked. Machines do listen to desperate entreaties. Dijan gave me the lowdown on the recently concluded war with the Maoists. Now that the Maoists have won the elections, let's hope they do the right thing by the people. As usual, the poor had borne the brunt of the conflict. It's a beautiful country with wonderful people. I hope they make it without further bloodshed.

The Himalayan Enfielders are a garage-cum-club. It's in the middle of the town and a busy place. Bikes roaring in and out the whole day. Vintage bikes vie for attention with the latest Enfield models. Groups of young and the not-so-young discuss their machines and the journeys that they had made, all day long. The boys took me under their wing quickly. I was one of their own.

The Israeli embassy is just behind the garage. I wonder how they work in there, what with the continuous cacophony of roaring bikes and horns. These boys couldn't care less. It was a blast seeing the bleak looks they fetched from the beady-eyed security guys. Some of the bikers were high on dope and beer. Fasouki, the head mechanic, insisted I put a hooter—a loud horn—on for the highway. I bowed to superior wisdom. He and his gang did a bang-up job on the bike over a couple of days. I shared a karmic beer with him.

Goofy is the type of guy who grows on you. I swear that's what everyone calls him. He was my contact with the Enfielders. Crazy-looking cat with far-out spectacles. Rides a 500-cc with the sangfroid of a psycho. I met him in the middle of the day when the sun was bright, and Goofy was not at his best. He shakes, he stirs, and he feels the rush of life beneath his wheels only as the evening hours approach. The entire gang from the club walked to a small joint for beer and momos. Fine. Then walked a few more steps into a nude dance bar. Cool. The crowd was getting drunk and raucous. Goofy signalled to me and we split from the crowd. I thanked my luck: I was to get an early night after all.

Yeah, right! Before I knew it we had hit three different dance bars, including one where traditional Nepali folk songs were performed. I was captive because I was riding pillion. By midnight we were at Thamel, where the tourists play, eating omelettes in buns on the roadside. This was the street of the gay people and we were being seriously ogled. Goofy gate-crashed into a marriage party and we had a few free drinks. I finally got him to leave me at the Hyatt casino, within walking distance of Joey's home. Hallelujah! I won that night. A tidy sum. I sang my way to Joey's house at four in the morning, all the while throwing stones at the stray dogs that showed their resentment of my singing.

The next morning was shopping-time. Raincoat, protective pants, cover for the saddlebags, a face mask and another pair of goggles. All this gear was from a shop which was a biker's delight. Goofy offered another night on the town. I politely declined.

The ride to Pokhara was breathtaking, too. There are natural geographical formations on the way which are awesome. It's a six-hour casual drive, but it had its excruciating moments. All the excesses of Kathmandu caught me in the middle of the road. I had the runs, and I had nowhere to go. That stretch of the road had a mountain on one side and the river on the other. I twitched uneasily on my seat, so desperate that I contemplated letting go on an as-is-where-is basis. Till an oasis beckoned in the form of a rundown hotel with a dirty bathroom. I just made it dirtier. Heady with relief, I got into conversation with Ram Avtar Gupta, a chanawallah. I sat and ate chana on the roadside and swapped stories. Me about my karmic fuck-ups, he about his. Ram and I, we were friends for a brief spell.

Vijay Subba is a great friend, and a thorough professional. He is the general manager of the Shangri-La

Village Resort at Pokhara. He and his pals took me for another night out, Nepal-style. Dance bars, casinos, massage parlours and tons to drink. The night life of Nepal is racy. By comparison, India is staid. When will the Indian government re-examine its archaic laws on obscenity, gaming and entertainment?

The middle-class morality of India is killing the tourist potential of the country. No amount of shouting 'Incredible India!' on televisions around the world is going to change that fact. You can't expect a tourist to have a government-regulated bed-time. Which in fact we do impose. The statistics speak for themselves and even a small nation like Thailand has many more visitors than this behemoth of a country. With very good reason.

While I was sitting in the open-air restaurant of Shangri-La Village, a stranger sidled up to me. I discovered he was an old college buddy, Anshuman, and we were meeting after twenty-five years or so. We chewed the old times apart. Had to meet him here of all places. Felt younger for a while. But only for a while. Then felt older, much, much older. How the years fly by. I'll never get used to the fact that most of the people I meet are younger than me.

College days are a blur of hazy memories. I used to be high on smack and a pretty vicious specimen, not the kind you'd think would make friends and influence people. Long hair, straggly beard, dirty jeans and a dazed expression was my signature look. The hostel room was a blast of music and acrid cigarette smoke. Started the day with lunch. No classes. Had, amazingly, a steady stream of girlfriends, including a nympho. She was the only girl who'd been through our entire gang of friends, one after the other till, one fine, grass-enhanced day, she casually asked me to screw her. I obliged, and went on obliging her for quite a while. My circle of college friends pays her homage every time we meet. Poons, wherever you are, we salute you. These are the sort of memories that pop up when you meet old college buddies.

Pokhara to Bhairava was a good ride. There was some sort of strike going on and the roads were empty. Fortunately, I was not harassed by the strikers and was allowed to pass through the barricades. Tourists are treated with a lot of respect in Nepal. I thought I was making good time when another Enfield roared past. Ridden by a guy with a blond pigtail. He was doing at least 120 kmph.

Had a bit of an accident myself. I hit a fellow on a cycle and he took a nasty toss. I barely managed to stay upright. He refused all help. Said he was all right and claimed he was at fault. You do meet the strangest people on the road. Any other man would have demanded money and hurled abuses at me. I shudder to think what would have happened if the blond pigtail had a collision with anyone.

Bhairava is a town on the way to Lumbini, the birthplace of the Buddha. By the time I had checked into a hotel in Bhairava and reached Lumbini, the main shrine was closed. I sat outside, meditated and prayed. There was a splatter of rain. '*Chinlap*' in our language means a good sign, a good omen, and rain signifies a blessing of the deities. Right then I knew that I would come to no harm on this trip.

Lumbini is not very well developed. Thank heavens for that. It still maintains some peace and quiet.

Fourteen hours along 600-plus kilometres from Bhairava to Rudrapur, in Uttarakhand state in India. This part of the road in Nepal is excellent and passes through dense forests. On the Indian side of the border there was a drunken monkey in human form making catcalls from a parapet on the bridge. He was with his gang of drunken pals and was into harassing the simple Nepalis who cross the border. Typical riff-raff of the north Indian plains. After a hard ride I was in no mood to brook this crap. I got off the bike, hurling the kind of Hindi invective I specialized in, in college. It was met with shock. Instead of a meek and cowed-down Nepali, the man had come up against an abusive Hindustani. He and his companions backed off, and fast. Feeling like a warrior and a fool at the same time, I split quickly. I had broken one of the cardinal rules I had set for myself: Don't get into hassles with locals. Foolish, foolish, foolish.

Rudrapur is a nondescript small town like the thousands that dot this part of the world. Dusty and dirty. I hunkered down for the night in a little hotel outside the main town. I was the only guest and a VIP. This was an important lesson I learnt on my journey. Stay in the smaller hotels outside town because you will always get a room. It will be cheaper than the central places, and you will be treated well by the staff.

Nevertheless, after the hospitality of south India and Nepal, and the experience at the border, I felt like an outsider in north India. Then I shook off the feeling, telling myself I was being paranoid, and generalizing to boot. I shook off the biases. One monkey was not going to spoil my fun. I was right. There were no unsavoury incidents on the road during my run in the northern plains.

10

I'm really into Begnas. The place where I am staying was previously known as 'Yogi Bari', meaning the 'the field of yogis'. This was where holy men did their penance and meditation. There is even a graveyard for them. The place vibrates with power and the aura is overwhelming. Am I being too dramatic? Leopards and yogis and the lazy God, all put together in one heady cocktail.

Once in a while, I buy Mohan, the caretaker, a bottle of the local *rakshi*. This is a potent brew of millet. Then it's party time for the indolent divine and his wife. His wife is a taciturn woman who looks much older than her forty-five years. After six children and a hard life, she treats herself to alcohol and cigarettes. When the bottle comes out, her personality flowers, and Mohan starts to cringe. His wife grows garrulous and starts to sing. Surprisingly nice voice she has, too. The children gather around the winter campfire, and roasted potatoes become the delicacy of the hour. More on this family later.

My plans after getting back to India were fluid, to say the least. I was truly a vagabond. The mind wandered from Delhi to Manali to Shimla and then to a hundred other places. I decided to head for Mussoorie in Uttarakhand. It is a beautiful hill station, past its prime. Too many tourists have taken their toll on the hillside. The old roads cannot take the traffic anymore. Even on a motorcycle, the going was slow.

I was headed to the Lal Bahadur Shastri National Academy of Administration. This is ,the training ground of the Indian Administrative Service where probationers are hounded by lessons for two years. It was the first time I was coming here after my own initial training. Normally, officers come either to lecture the inmates or to attend short refresher courses themselves. I did neither. The infrastructure was a hell of a lot better, yet it somehow felt the same. My host was a Kerala-cadre officer, Manoj Kumar, who was the deputy director of the Academy. I roared into his quarters, dirty and dishevelled.

It had been a 300-kilometre ride through Haridwar and Dehra Dun. The traffic jam at Haridwar was killing. Some major Hindu festival was on and devotees from the plains had thronged there to celebrate it. Mind-boggling. I suspect the traffic policemen just give up after a while. Some old pal from the past cracked my rearlights in the jam. Nothing major ensued. We eyed each other, smiled, shrugged and carried on with our lives.

Manoj gave me a 'Comfortable Screw', a cocktail of

vodka, orange juice and Southern Comfort. Whew! That was a cracking cocktail. Followed by delicious Malabar biryani cooked by Maya, his lovely wife. The surprise gifts on the road come at unexpected times and places. Manoj is erudite, extremely well-read and has a degree in engineering from the Indian Institute of Technology. God knows what he is doing in the bureaucracy.

Despite the chaos during daytime, Mussoorie is worth a walk in the morning. I took a stroll around the Academy and had tea with the trainers. I don't know if I am wrong but the majority of trainers have a streak of cruelty in them. To get around the modern-day prohibition of corporal punishment, they devise other, more subtle means of torture. During my time there I was denied leave to attend a sister's wedding in Delhi, while some well-connected probationers visited the capital regularly. Sycophancy was a subject perhaps not taught but certainly practised. One of the bandicoots of that time had given me a year to be hanged by the people of Kerala. Hey Tootsie! I'm still alive and kicking. 'Kicking' being the operative word if you come near me.

Then there'd been the batchmates. I'd got along well with them for the most part, except with a few. There was this bunch of holier-than-thou social reformers. They thought they knew the path to India's salvation. They did not get to do much for the country, but they're doing fine, I hear. One of the faults of recruitment to the government services in the civil sector is the lack of a psychological profile for candidates. I was probably not programmed to be a government servant myself. Crooks, megalomaniacs and people like me should be identified and weaned out at the interview itself.

It was a great day for me when I met the legendary Ruskin Bond and his good friend Ganesh Saili. I served a couple of drinks to Bond, in Saili's house. I apologized to the others because my jeans had gravy stains on them and that was the cleanest outfit in my possession that day. Ruskin has a twinkle in his eye when he talks sexy, even at this age. I can imagine the blaze in his youth. Surprisingly down-to-earth and extremely witty, he immediately saw me for the rascal that I am. Humility, graciousness and wisdom equal Ruskin Bond. Mr Bond lives in Landour, in Mussoorie, and is a bachelor who fondly remembered the cheap whisky he used to drink in his youth before he hit the big time. I drink good whisky even though I'm yet to hit the big time. Maybe that's where I go wrong; I should have stuck to the rum I drank in my youth. Ganesh is a cool cat and an excellent host, with a very gracious wife.

Rudra Gangadharan, a senior colleague from Kerala, heads the Academy as its director. He is pretty relaxed for a babu. And I like him a lot, especially as he invited me for a round of drinks at his residence.

Then there was Kishen Lal, the head waiter who worked for a stunning forty-four years in the Academy. I had arrived there just to be present at his farewell, or so it seemed to me. There was a group of scientists on a training programme, and Ashok, their course coordinator, and another friend of mine, wanted me to give them a talk. I agreed, with the proviso that it would be in the evening with at least beer to go around. Imagine a group of scientists interacting with an ex-bureaucrat with gravy stains on his jeans. Sometimes, the weirdest people hit it off—and this was a one-of-a-kind day for me. We took some photographs, we had some beer, we shared some jokes and we contributed a small fund of Rs 8,000 for Kishen Lal who was retiring that day. One of the scientists told me, unaccountably, that I was 'sucking the fly in the milk of life'. Figure that one out yourself.

This trip to Mussoorie was a closure of sorts. The last time I was there I was ready to imprint my stamp on the Indian public life. This time I came back sealed, stamped and delivered by the same. The full circle. More like the full Monty.

11

Bilaspur is a small town in Himachal Pradesh I entered in the night. Head constable Manohar is a dashing young man who boxes. I met him at an accident site just an hour away from Bilaspur. It was dark, and traffic was at a standstill. I crept along the side of the road and there was confusion galore. I noticed this young man in civilian clothes taking charge of things. He came to me and said that if I gave him a ride to town he would get me through the mess. I broke another rule that day ('no hitchhikers') and agreed to give him a lift. I had had a long day travelling from Mussoorie via Shimla to this place, and besides, I sized the bugger up and he didn't look like a highwayman.

As he'd promised, he got me through the traffic somehow and we pelted downhill. The man suffered from verbal diarrhoea, boasting about his boxing prowess and his other athletic feats. He followed that up with the advice not to pick up strangers in the night.

The ride was lengthy and tiring. Some stretches of the road looked like they had been carpet-bombed. Shimla had been considered for a night halt but I was sick of hideous concrete buildings on mountainsides. The bike had also been having some electrical problems which were temporarily fixed at Solan, a place at one time famous for its beer. I did not know I had an appointment with head constable Manohar, about to be promoted shortly to assistant sub-inspector of police.

The fellow arranged an indifferent hotel and wanted to give me dinner. He had been to Sikkim and out-boxed everyone there. Getting rid of a grateful policeman is no mean feat. Actually, we're more used to policemen who want something from you and not the other way around. It was quite unnerving. I even considered the possibility that the chap was gay. Finally, as a compromise, we exchanged telephone numbers and he treated me to a cold drink outside his house. He thought I was a cardamom farmer and introduced me as one to his whole locality. He could have taught a thing or two to a limpet. Or maybe he just liked me.

Manohar's hotel of choice was one of the dirtiest I have stayed in through the entire journey. You know when dirt has seeped into the woodwork and the fabric themselves. That was the better part. The food looked bad and tasted worse. I have thought long and hard about what I ate and I can't figure out what it was. This cook could spoil an egg. My dues to Manohar are paid in full.

Many friends had told me garbled stories about a village full of Israelis up in some remote corner of Himachal Pradesh. Even some of the local people were not aware of it. I had finally pinpointed it as the twin villages of Pulga and Tulga. There is a popular Sikh shrine called Manikaran on the way. Hundreds of devotees seem to go there. One interesting aspect was the number of young pilgrims on motorcycles, sporting flags. The dirt road ended in a one-mouse town called Barsiyani.

The bike had to be parked there. I paid someone to watch over it and walked half-an-hour uphill to Pulga, with a porter. Pulga-Tulga is picturesque, to say the least, framed against a juniper forest. Small wooden houses with a few rooms to let. There are also some two-storeyed houses which form the luxury segment, charging a hundred rupees a day. Everything is very basic and that is where the fun lies. The place is full of long-term tourists. The rooms were terrible and I finally landed at the last lodge in town. It was also the biggest. A three-storeyed timber monster. 'Uncleji' was the man in charge—or so I thought.

Uncleji was a thin, gaunt, mustachioed character with watery eyes and a weak personality. He was the owner but the wife was the boss. Thick-set, heavy and with a brooding, sombre personality. There was no contest between the two. She eyed me suspiciously and wanted the money in advance. The money and my Hindi softened her considerably. I observed that when any of her would-be clients declined to forward an advance, she demanded to see their passports. Clearly having suffered at the hands of some of her guests, she was severely lacking in the trust department. But with my money in her pocket, she almost smiled at me.

A small canteen composed of tarpaulin above and seats on the ground served great Israeli cuisine. I wiped up great quantities of hummus and tahini with soft pita bread. Uncleji's pet dog ate only onion soup. Weird. The inhabitants were almost all charas and ganja addicts. It was like a scene from Woodstock. Flower children with their chillums. And me with my bottle of vodka. I had no one to share it with so I called Uncleji over for a toast. He came and sipped hesitantly at the liberal shot I'd poured him. He was a slow and sparing drinker and I was surprised. The next evening, when I invited him across for a drink, he literally ran away, keeping well out of sight till I retired to bed. He was a smoker all right, but clearly not used to alcohol. He must have suspected that two days in a row would be lethal for him, because he never emerged again from his strategic retreat.

The cooks and the waiters were very professional. They migrated with the tourist seasons everywhere. Winters in Goa, summers in Himachal—that sort of thing. What they omitted to tell me is that they all smoked too. The Nepali porter who carried my saddlebags informed me that a large quantity of ganja is planted in the forest and a brisk trade goes on. A part of the dope trail now, but it has a history as well. As usual, the British had been the first outsiders to locate this beautiful place, and a forest bungalow stands testimony to the fact. A walk around the forest trails and the small waterfalls is stimulating—the perfect getaway for young couples. And for lovers of solitude such as I.

Uncleji's hotel had a very queer common bathroom. There were large windows on all sides without window panes or curtains. Your activities were not too private. I wonder who the peeping Tom in the family was—Uncleji or Auntyji?

Night time was filled with the sounds of rhythmic lovemaking on a creaking wooden bed, on a creaking wooden floor which happened to be my ceiling. The doped-out couple, whoever they were, were patently having an extended ball. No wonder Uncleji is a junkie and looks mortally afraid of Auntyji. The pressure of being compared with, and all that jazz.

Gwendolyn and Gertrude from the United States paired up at their place of stay. My first close-up of a lesbian couple. Without the sexual tension, they were lovely company, although their constant kissing made me a little uncomfortable. I learnt to modestly avert my eyes every time it happened. The Israelis and other foreigners outnumber the locals two to one at least. This place does not look like a part of India. But the view is great, the food is great, the dope is great and the company is way out.

12

Pulga to Manali, on the highway to Chandigarh, is a touristy ride and the way is littered with restaurants of all shapes and sizes. Kullu town is famous for some of its festivals and especially for its shawls. There is this five-kilometre tunnel which is badly lit and filled with car fumes, where a motorcyclist can get disoriented. But that's part of the thrill.

Landed up in Manali where the tourist season had just about ended. This town is the playground of the Chandigarh and Delhi crowd. The hillside is dotted with all types of hotels. The main bazaar is small and the usual shops selling knick-knacks to tourists abound. The drainage is in a mess and when it rains the refuse of the town pours into the main street. The surrounding areas of the town have developed and some nice cottages are available on hire. I had arrived a day earlier than I was expected, but the waiter working in the cottage where I was to stay very graciously agreed to arrange a room for me in another cottage nearby.

I found out in time that most of these fellows are from Delhi and are crooks. They planned to charge me a whopping three thousand bucks for a night. I told them to shove it, and found a place for myself. I found this to be a constant problem during my stay in Manali. The outsiders who come to this place to earn a living are looking for a fast buck. Whether it is the local paanwallah, the barber, the shopkeeper or the cabbies, all are out to squeeze you.

Spent the evening in the old section of the town. This has narrow roads and is populated by backpacking foreigners. The hotels are basic but the ambience and the food are excellent. There are groups of people having a good time. I joined an American group who had a couple of guitars between them. Music makes it easy to make friends. Jimbo and friends were a delight to be with for a night. They were in their thirties, but we knew a few songs in common, the 1960s and '70s classics. Nowadays it's harder and harder to find people who recognize your favourites. The bakeries on this side of town are fabulous. Mouth-watering fare if you know where to look.

The place I stayed in for a night was closing shop the next day. It was a cottage, on the Simsa road, taken on lease by Pradeep who runs a dhaba in one of the shadier spots of Delhi. Fascinating story of a boy from rural Bengal who ran away from home to make it in the mean streets of 'Dilli'. He has a yearly arrangement with the owner of the cottage and leases it for three months for a hundred thousand rupees. He makes a profit of about the same amount. We spoke a few lines in Bengali and he threw in a 'fish-fry' free of charge.

I leased a cottage from the helpful Vijay of Manali, a charming and shrewd businessman. This was to be my home for the next year, I told myself. I would travel around and keep returning here for rest and some writing. How was I to know, then, that the plans we make are just ripples in the water? I spent a week getting the cottage ready for habitation. I stocked up on provisions, repaired the bike and did the things you do when at home. I had no servants and had to cook and clean. I went on a fast for a few days and meditated regularly. For four days I walked around in the nude inside the house. Just to see how it felt. The habit of a lifetime comes into play and the hands invariably slide to cover the privates. I cured myself of that habit. What benefit I derived from that is anybody's guess.

Grandpop's is where I shopped. If I went to any other shop he would look at me accusingly with his doggy eyes. Thakur, the Cro-Magnon, had introduced me to this Shylock on my first visit here. He made a lot of money out of me. But the stuff was good. His homemade cheese was worth every penny.

The cottage I took transpired to be some sort of public park. People strolled in and out as if they owned the place. Some boys even asked me for some drinking water, like I was a waiter. Maybe I looked like one. One day in the IAS and the next day serving water to unknown ruffians. As a villainous cousin said, I'd asked for it. One day, a young beggar woman walked in demanding money and would not leave till I gave her something. Even the local dogs began to harass me. They pinched a shoe of mine and left it behind the outhouse.

The place came with an orchard. At plucking time, people had a picnic in my courtyard. I couldn't figure out those people. I was in a new place and kept a low profile. Peering at everything from behind curtains, in the nude. Perhaps if they had seen me in that condition, they would have left me alone. Potbelly and all.

The monsoon season was giving of its best and that was one of my prime reasons for staying put. Lashing rain and an Andhra breakfast in the Himachal hills. The fellow from Andhra Pradesh who was now serving me could only speak broken Hindi. Surreal. The locals said that the rainfall was too heavy and the summer too hot. Same old climate-change gripe. We've fucked up nature big time and now we must pay the price. I cannot understand the reluctance of the big business lobby—especially in the United States—to acknowledge the problem and to take steps in concert with the rest of the world. Those guys are going to get rid of the human species one way or the other. By climate change or nuclear holocaust.

There were actually *packs* of dogs in town, roaming about pretty aggressively. I suspected it was because of the method of garbage disposal, or rather the absence of any such thing. There was enough to eat, live and be merry on for those dogs. The same went for the crows.

Suraj came regularly to massage me. He was from Haryana state, migrating to Manali for six months a year.

His massage was of the rural variety and on the rougher side. He lived in his own tent in a paddy-field, paying a rent of a hundred and fifty a month. There were many others like him. I went to have roti and subzi in Suraj's tent. Food just enough to get by on. That's India for you.

Kurum Dut was a travel agent who specialized in motorcycle tours. He had a stable of more than fifteen Enfield bikes with a garage and a mechanic. He also had a plain-Jane Danish girlfriend whom he liked to show off. The sound of the Thunderbird is a bit muted. Every mechanic I met on the road wanted me to put the old-style silencer on. This time I capitulated and a blast of the old, deep sound greeted me when I went to collect my bike from Kurum's garage. He agreed to take me to Leh in August, together with a group of Germans.

One of the things that fascinated me about those denizens of Manali was their capacity for ball-breaking drinking. Every time I watched them in action provided a revelation. Was it a conspiracy to impress me? Pampu, Doctor and Vijay revealed their heroic capacities once again before my astounded eyes. Bottle after bottle disappeared with great rapidity. I began to see them as kegs of whisky. Forced myself out of hallucinating.

Went up to the Rohtang Pass. Just to try out the bike. On the way I passed the 'Ministry of Chicken', a rundown eatery. The only thing impressive about it was the name. The owner sure had a sick sense of humour.

The rains were beginning to ease, or so I thought. There was work to be attended to at home and I was summoned back to Sikkim. I left Manali early in the morning and headed for Delhi, 667 kilometres away. The rains caught me early on and it was slow going. A drizzle in the dark, with fog thrown in, are not the best of riding conditions. Daylight brought some relief. It was an uneventful ride, with good, authentic Punjabi food on the way. My longest ride so far, a full fifteen hours on the road with food and piss breaks in between.

The bike acted up again—some problem with the electrical circuit—and kept stalling. I got to my destination somehow and crashed out. Next day, the bike refused to start altogether and I kissed it in gratitude. It had carried me to Delhi before dying on me. I made arrangements for a thorough overhaul, through Chauhan, a friend and himself an avid Enfielder.

On the border of Delhi, two bulky motorcycle-borne cops ran circles around my bike, watching me carefully. I anticipated a shakedown but found to my surprise that they were merely looking over the bike and the gear. They gave me a thumbs-up and went their way. These things happen on the roads. No biker is too old nor tired to be interested in other people's bikes.

13

The detour to my home state was not a scheduled break in the journey. I was receiving compensation for some ancestral property acquired by the government of Sikkim.

A word about the power projects being signed out in Sikkim. The state has enormous power potential for its size, and that could have been judiciously used as a resource for generating revenue for both the government as well as the local stakeholders. As usual, other considerations were more important. The Government of India needed power to fuel the rampaging economy. The private power-generating companies had enormous clout and a full kitty to have their way. The greedy politicians needed only short-term benefits and the bureaucrats happily went along with their schemes.

There has been a serious, sustained effort by the indigenous Lepcha community to fight against some projects in their homeland of Dzongu, a protected reserve. They have been peacefully and patiently petitioning both the central and the state governments for a solution but to no avail. A hunger-strike has been going on for more than 250 days at the time of writing. The 'Affected Citizens of Teesta' is the hastily put-together, non-government body spearheading this movement. This is a losing fight and the people in power will just ignore the agitating aboriginals. Who follows the Gandhian approach in India today?

I was going home to receive compensation for some land taken over for one of these projects. The money was welcome since I was jobless, but the way it came was not the right way. In the office where the cheques were being distributed, there was this callow idiot of a private power company employee. I was expressing my anguish at the way things were going and he butted into our conversation, justifying their doings in our land. He barely got away with his life. Having been a bureaucrat is a help at times. I may have been too cynical to take on the state and central governments on the issue, but scaring that creep witless was the best that I could do.

I think I have disappointed some of the people I respect by not joining the agitation. It was a heart-wrenching choice. But this time of my life was for me and for nobody else. I had left a secure job to find a new path. I wanted to have nothing to do with matters of governance any more. The law of nature embodies impermanence and change. This decision of the government to go ahead with the power projects will forever change the demography and the culture of north Sikkim. Maybe that was an intended consequence—or maybe it was not. I have turned my back and walked away from my people. Not that I could have done much.

Menda's friends wanted to meet me and I called them home for dinner. A first cocktail was offered and all relished it. A second was also guzzled down pretty efficiently. I am beginning to get a handle on my daughter and her friends.

Menda had an offer to go abroad through a Rotarian friend in an exchange programme. The place was Alaska— of all the places in the world. I leapt at the offer and so did she. This would mean a year's setback in her studies, but so what? A chance of a lifetime cannot be ignored. I believe that the role of a parent is to help children find their real goal, their passion, in life. If this is achieved nothing more needs to be done. Gifted children follow their own path. The present system of education does not allow for searching out one's path. It is hidebound and time-bound. Menda will be allowed to find out how work becomes play for her throughout her life. We are not afraid to let her go.

We are not afraid, either, of the matter of the birds and the bees. Dechen, even as the youngest in the family, used to delight in comparing Menda's growing breasts to various fruit. Of course, it started from a fried egg, but went on to lemons, oranges, mangoes ... you get the picture. Dechen, when her time came, casually mentioned to me that she had had her first menstrual cycle. Now it's her turn for the fruits but she brazens it out. I sometimes wonder if I did things the right way but the girls seem okay with it.

14

Sonam Paljor Denjongpa's father-in-law thinks he's eccentric. So does everyone else. Picked up by the Chogyal of Sikkim in the 1970s and sent on scholarship to the Brown College in Massachusetts, he wore monk's robes in college. He went on a date with a white Anglo-Saxon Protestant and told her that some day she would be his wife. She slapped him for his temerity. She also later married him. Maria is now a white Anglo-Saxon Buddhist.

Sonam came back to Sikkim and started a school with a vision to make the kids think, with other like-minded people, but was hounded out of the country as a potential threat to national integration. It was the time Sikkim had just merged with India and the government was paranoid. Sonam does not mince his words and with an American wife in tow, he was easy meat for the cloak-and-dagger boys. Back to the United States and a life of struggle. Finally, he and his wife set up a high-end catering company in Boston. Put two sons through college.

His lifelong dharma mentor is His Holiness Dodrupchen Rimpoche, a renowned master of the Nyingmapa sect of Buddhism. Sonam has been a follower his entire life and is currently serving the Rimpoche as his right-hand man.

I got to know him when I was in Gangtok during my days there in the government. We performed the Lama Gondue, a puja for world peace and brotherhood. The Rimpoche had selected the Ringhim monastery to conduct it in. This monastery is in Mangan, my ancestral place. More than 300 monks from all over Sikkim participated in the ten-day prayer ceremony, which is still held annually. A school for monks has also been set up in the same monastery. All this is under the guidance and direction of the Rimpoche. Sonam is the monk who goes around getting people like me to organize the lay side of things.

Then came the day a building belonging to the royal family of Sikkim was to be leased out as a hotel to me. I was still in government service and could not do business in my name. Sonam willingly gave his name to carry out the entire business, signing blank cheques over to me. The bank was taking its time and then help came from an unexpected source. His Holiness called me and gave me 20,00,000 rupees, interest-free. He laughed when I talked of signing a document. No document was ever signed but the burden of that debt was the heaviest I have ever felt. This is the sacred bond as taught to me by the action of the Rimpoche. This is the sacred bond as taught to me by the action of Sonam, his student. This is Thamzhi at work.

I could return only a few lakhs and the guilt was overwhelming. Then, when I got the money for the land acquired from me by the government, the first thing I did was to pay back the Master. What a relief. What joy in paying back a loan!

Sonam wears his hair long. Ponytail and crimson robes. When he goes for his yearly sabbatical to the United States, he comes back looking clean and fresh. After a month in the monastery he's back to being his Bhutia best: dirty and dishevelled. He is in the habit of yawning in the face of anyone he finds boring. Or looking at the ceiling or outside the window while that person is talking to him. Then, he abruptly walks out of the room. Eccentric? You bet!

His partner in serving the Rimpoche, Sonam Wangdi Bhutia, better known as Babula, is an engineer with the state government. After years of doing odd jobs for the Master, he approached him with the request to be taught something special, some mantras. He was told to work, work and work some more. That was his role for this life. Despite his initial dejection, he took three years' leave without pay and went to work building a statue of the patron saint of Sikkim, Padmasambhava. It is a 108-foot statue at a place called Samduptse in Sikkim. This was a project overseen by the Rimpoche, and his two loyal Sonams did all the work. Below budget and before time. It happens even in India.

Babula has been a widower for more than a decade now and I have never seen him so much as look at a woman. I wonder at these people who've seen the world but manage to retain such purity of thought and action, in their devotion to their Guru, and towards each other. I have learnt a lot by being part of their circle. But I am a rascal and that's that.

My relationship with Pema of Netuk House is an unusual one. We work together on various projects initiated by Sonam, the monk, but we don't meet very frequently. He is special to me because when I was sick the first time, he came to my house with a copy of the prayer '*Ri Wo Sang Cho*', the one called the diamond practice I engaged in, later, on the road. This was revealed in Sikkim to Namkha Jigmed, a master practitioner, by the *dakinis*, who are divine female spirits, as the practice which would open the gates to the secret land of Shangri-La. You have to be taught to do it by a qualified master. I really don't know how it works or if it works at all. All I can say from my experience is that I feel peace and a sense of having actively participated in things not normally allowed to chaps like us.

15

I flew back to Delhi to continue my interrupted journey. The bike had been repaired and I'd missed it. This constant movement is like an addiction. I was hooked, line and sinker.

It was during this visit to Delhi that I met the unforgettable barber, who took me under his wing, and decided for himself what kind of shave and haircut I really needed.

Then there was that cross-eyed mechanic in Chandigarh. I was getting a bushelful of great personalities on this particular trip. I wanted him to merely tighten the screws in the back carrier which had started to rattle somewhat. He was a garrulous chap and fired questions at me non-stop. I'd grown used to people asking me questions on the road and I answered as truthfully as possible. I only avoided saying I was in the IAS to avoid being lynched. This man was different. His questions were probing and personal. What does your wife do? How many children do you have? Is your wife beautiful? How much money do you make? How tall is your wife? What does your brother do? Are you in love with your wife? You see the trend of his questions; every second question was about the wife, which, in our country, is tantamount to talking about sex. That guy was a special pervert. Despite my initial irritation, I was amused by his desperation to know all. I began shamelessly lying to him. The taller my stories, the greater his greed for knowledge. My wife became a combination of the finest actresses of Bollywood and Hollywood. She was from a filthy-rich family. She gave me five sons in a row, a thing prized by men in Punjab. Those sort of lies. He finally caught on and started preaching to me on the evils of lying and betraying trust. To be lectured by a pervert on the sins of lying and breach of trust was a special treat. He was still ranting as I scooted off. I think he was insane, but he did a good job on the bike. Only, the screws on my carrier weren't the only ones around that needed to be tightened.

I 'overnighted' at Chandigarh in the house of Balwant, an engineer. Balwant suffers from a variety of ailments, including diabetes and high blood pressure. He makes it a point to sleep early for reasons of health. Sharp at nine at night, as he said. I was impressed with his discipline. The catch was that he would get roaring drunk before he went to sleep. I failed to understand his logic.

Reached Manali without incident. I was supposed to get ready for the dazzling ride to Leh. A last-minute check up of the motorcycle was a must because on that stretch of road there would be hardly any settlements, leave alone a mechanic, or, for that matter, petrol, which I found out through bitter experience.

During the course of my preparation I was honoured with a visit by the local income-tax inspector. Let me tell you about this low-level functionary of the central government. A huge number of them are petty thieves who go around their jurisdiction bullying minor businessmen. This charlie knew that the cottage I was in was being used as a hotel for a few months in the year. He rang the doorbell authoritatively, gave me the eye and asked to see the manager. My dress sense after leaving the service had turned so bohemian that he mistook me for the cook. To be fair to the man, I was in shorts and a vest and had not combed my longish hair. I told him that I had rented the cottage for a year. Despite the obvious scepticism on his face, he reluctantly agreed to believe me, and then proceeded to question me as he would a tax-evader. I had had enough of being polite to the bully. He even had a henchman behind him, who kept dumb, regarding me with a fishy-eyed look. Maybe he was being trained in the art of bullying.

That was when I pulled the old IAS rabbit out of the hat. They swayed like reeds in a thunderstorm, refused to give me their names and ran for their lives. My abuses chased them right up to the gate. Victory, in small skirmishes with petty government servants, is sweet, indeed. I relish each one and chalk it up as one more blow on behalf of the suffering masses.

Kurum's garage is in the old section of Manali. I used to hang around while the mechanic did his bit on the bike. With nothing better to do, you watch the tourists go by— or you watch dogs rutting. There was this one time when two males were after a single bitch, causing a ruckus on the road. The antics were such that at one point it looked like one of the dogs was getting a blow job. A local bystander piped up with the opinion that this was the influence of tourists.

I was waiting for the Germans to arrive and was raring to go. The stretch of road we planned to take was one on which serious bikers from all over the world came to ride religiously. D-day was tomorrow.

16

Getting up early is not a problem for me, and at 7.30 sharp, I was at the appointed place, the garage. Only the mechanic and a driver were there. These biking expeditions to inhospitable terrain are accompanied by a mechanic with spare parts and other provisions, including petrol, in a four-wheel vehicle. The driver was a taciturn Ladhaki.

I treated the two men to an early morning breakfast. Eat when you can is another mantra on the road. Breakfast did not move the Ladhaki but the cigarette did the trick. He smiled shyly. The amazing thing was that both the gentlemen were prepared to pay for the food. I felt we were on to a good start, although it was 8.30 and no action had begun. Finally, I rang up Kurum who said he'd sent word to me through somebody that we were starting only in the afternoon. Fuck! But I wasn't about to wait. So, knowing that a party was coming behind me, I gunned the old roadster and off we went.

Past the sicko and his Ministry of Chicken joke. The Rohtang Pass, with its tiny shops selling noodles, and renting out mules to giggling tourists ready for a ride. The way from Manali to Rohtang has some weird rock formations right on the roadside. Particularly impressive is a huge rock shaped like a conch. There is even a bloody house right at its base. The chap living there is not normal. That's for sure.

I could see another couple on an old Enfield ahead of me. That was Chris and Samantha from the UK, rocking in this part of the world. They were a young unmarried couple who had hooked up for the time of their lives. I caught up with them when Samantha had gone behind the bushes and the standing bike fell on top of Chris. I stopped to offer help. Now, I know nothing about bikes but one has one's pride and it is the code of the road. Chris had been trying to straighten out the mudguard which had bent a little and had been creating a problem on the turns. The bike fell down during his amateur efforts to mend the thing. The experienced old biker then took charge and we set it right. With effusive thanks ringing in my ears and my own friendly word of advice to the youngsters, I zoomed away.

The major part of the first day's journey was on a dirt road. Dust was aplenty but it was the bumps that were the problem. Bone-jarring stuff. All along the way, apples were being collected on the roadside for transportation to the plains. Chris was ahead but staying close to me. I paid him no heed, like an old hand on the road does. I had the better bike with the latest suspension—and I was getting hell from the road. I wondered about the kids, especially Samantha, riding pillion. But when you are young and horny, bumps on the road could add to the excitement.

Then Chris waved me down. He had a stalling problem. From the dim recesses of my memory from the time I had a similar bike in college, I remembered how cleaning the spark plug did the job, and made him do so. And, voila, he was roaring again. By now I was firmly entrenched in his mind as a mastermind. We stopped for lunch at a small settlement where we found a mechanic. Chris and Samantha were college kids. They were having fun. We Indians need similar freedom in our youth. Or we fetch up at forty-four, whooping it up like a boy on a bike.

After lunch, I quickly went my way because I had shot my bolt as far as the mechanics of a bike were concerned. I had to move quickly and these guys were slowing me down. There was no question that they were going to have further problems on the road. I told them a bunch of riders were following behind, with a mechanic in tow, and to wait for them in case of further trouble with their machine. These guys had each other and their lust for company. All I had was my wanderlust.

The journey uphill had begun, and there was no more population to be seen. Grasslands and no trees. Wild and getting wilder. Evening came, and in blazed a thunderstorm. In minutes the sky blackened, the rumblings began and the downpour set in, accompanied by a howling wind. The bike had to be slowed down to a crawl. Pretty frightening, actually. I was worried about the lightning as I felt like a sitting duck on the plateau.

Sharchu is a huddle of tents. The way those locals down below talked about Sharchu, you'd think it was a small town, at least. I was disappointed with the reality. Drenched, cold, hungry and tired, I was looking for warmth and a good night's rest. The solitary policeman at the outpost told me that I'd left the luxury tents back down the road behind me, now six kilometres the wrong way. Shit! Back again in the wind and the rain and running low on fuel. The cop had also told me there was no petrol to be had in Sharchu. And my companions-to-be hadn't shown up.

The 'luxury' tents were a misnomer. They did have attached and reasonably clean bathrooms, but running water existed only in theory. It was better to use the bucket and mug to catch the trickle that emerged. Having a bath in the cold was a desperate affair. The food was a coolie's dinner. Then a long night with the wind somehow finding its way between the sheets.

Early next morning I ignored the offer of a dog's breakfast and went looking for petrol and civilization. A foreign couple heading towards Manali were carrying jerrycans of petrol on their bike. I requested them for a few litres and was told to buzz off. Well, they got their karmic kick at me. Having stopped at the Waldorf Astoria of Sharchu and spent some money on breakfast, I enquired casually about the availability of petrol. The owner of the

Waldorf was also its cook, waiter, cleaner and receptionist, and he winked at me knowingly. He knew I was on the lookout—he'd heard it on the grapevine. (*Sucker ahoy!*) The policeman had lied to me the night before. The fucker's outpost was two feet away and he was actually having tea at the place I was. The dhaba owner looked me squarely in the eye and demanded an exorbitant hundred rupees a litre. No choice. Pay double the price or shudder to a halt on the road. To save face I hoped aloud that the petrol was not mixed with kerosene. For that comment I got a diatribe on the work and general ethics of the Waldorf establishment. But he also grandly admitted he could not be sure about the fellow from whom he'd bought the petrol. That's honesty for you.

Now, only '*Om Ah Hung Vajra Guru Padma Siddhi Hung*' can see me through. The simplest translation of this prayer to Padmasambhava is a reminder to him of his promise to help all sentient beings gain enlightenment. (I hope I'm not pilloried for my lousy translation.) It works. Dharma works.

Lovely day for a ride on the plateau. Clear skies and the sun had been up and about early in the morning. This was silent country and a bike was an intrusion. I felt truly sorry for the disturbance. An eagle kept me company for a long while. The ride through that cold and lovely desert played havoc, nevertheless, with your fair and lovely complexion.

I drove uphill to cross the Tatlangla Pass which, at a little over 17,000 feet, is supposed to be the second highest motorable pass in the world. Halfway up, the weather turned nasty, quick as a flash. One minute there was glorious sunshine and the next, a violent afternoon squall hit you in the face. Literally. The rain stung my skin. Worse, I began to be pelted with small hailstones. The rain gear was already on. The goggles came off, the visor came on and the face mask came up. The road had become slippery with the hailstones and it was bitingly cold. Thunder and lightning pursued me everywhere. Then I saw Shangri-La in the form of two forlorn tents in the middle of nowhere with a hand-painted wooden sign claiming the title of 'Hutel and Resturan'.

I skidded to a stop and stepped into the bigger tent. A thin Ladhaki with a Mongol moustache and scraggly beard smiled weakly at me. We brought in the gear together because the hailstones and the rain had increased in ferocity. The tent flapped wildly in the wind and I asked whether it would hold. My host surveyed the main pole and hoped all would be well. I was not too sure. This tent was one of the army parachute rejects which are sold to the public. Its thin fabric stretches to a diameter of about twenty feet. On one side of this tent lay the kitchen area, and there was a row of bench-beds around in a semi-circle with small tables in front. The tables and half the beds were the restaurant and the rest were the hotel.

This chap was a character. High-pitched voice emerging from a skinny body wearing an oversized army parka and dirty white snowshoes. An almost black weather-beaten face which hadn't seen a wash for weeks, or so it seemed to my feverish gaze. From the moment he laid eyes on me he started to talk, and kept on the litany for the one-and-a-half hours I was there. We spoke in Hindi, our national language, his more broken than mine. The incongruity of the situation did not escape me. A Ladakhi and a Sikkimese talking in Hindi. In the old days it would have been in some form of pidgin Tibetan.

He was from Leh and he ran this nowhere place for six months a year. The other six months he was snowbound. I got to know his family history, the history of the region, the migration of the outsiders, and the politics of religion there, the politics per se, the weather, the tourist trade, and many more things which I forget. I had to answer a barrage of questions about myself, my religion, my state, my family and many other things I am happy to forget.

It was a fixed-menu hotel and you ate what you got. I ordered lunch, a memory that stays with me. It was composed of cold rice, cold rajma and an indeterminate vegetable curry. More revolting than the fare was the way he served me. After putting the rice in a steel plate with the curries slopped onto the rice, he inspected a spoon. He was not satisfied with its hygiene and wiped it on a black greasy cloth which was hung from the parachute. A second inspection left him still unhappy and he picked up another spoon and repeated the procedure. Pleased with the result, he shoved the spoon in the rice and, with a winning smile, laid it on the table. All this drama was going on five feet in front of me. I hastily plucked the spoon out of the rice and washed it with mineral water.

But I could not wash the offered lunch. The moron had attempted to cook rajma at 17,000 feet. It is difficult to boil this hard bean even at sea level. I tried to eat the half-cooked result but my eyes would invariably stray to the black cloth which looked almost alive. So I gave up eating and hurt the Hindi-speaking Mongol's sentiments. He fussed, he enquired and he cajoled but I stood firm in my refusal to eat anymore of his garbage. He didn't speak to me for a full minute, clearly shocked. But these mountain men are hardy. They bounce back even in the face of major setbacks. He was back to his chirpy self soon after. I kept directing desperate looks at the sky, but nothing doing. I had to stay and bear it.

Then, someone similar, but younger, came in from the other tent, to assail me with his own brand of interrogation. I could barely take one of these chaps but two jokers at the same time, speaking bad Hindi, was too much. I bolted. Can you believe that the younger man requested me to stay to chat a little longer? Like I'd travelled an entire subcontinent for the privilege of being bored by two fruitcakes on a mountain top.

It was still raining but the hail had stopped. As a parting present, Squeaky Voice touchingly gave me a small, woollen, frighteningly dirty piece of rug to use as a saddle. The wet seat and the cold made me accept his loving gift.

I gingerly ran the bike in the middle of the road, trying to avoid the drifts of fallen hail. One mistake and I'd be kaput. The blessed rain kept on falling. It was only a couple more kilometres to the top. I was riding with the clouds but I did not love it. Thank God for my leather chaps; the legs were fine. But my fingers were freezing. I had just a pair of biker's half-gloves and I was experiencing hell in my digits. At one stage the pain was so excruciating that I stopped the bike, took out some face towels and wrapped them around my hands. While I was engaged in the task, I saw two cars of astonished tourists staring at me through their wound-up car windows.

I broke through the clouds to find myself on top of the pass, where the sun was shining and all was fine with the world. Those amazed tourists were there and wanted to take photographs of the towel-mittened man. One lady in particular cooed to me and called me brave, watched by her suspicious husband. I love it when nice-looking women coo at me.

The ride downhill was fast and then the bike started sputtering. Waldorf Astoria had done me in. The conman *had* mixed in kerosene. Cursing my own stupidity, and in the middle of nowhere, I glided downhill. The coughing continued for a few kilometres but then it cleared. Smooth again. The old bike did not let me down again. Nor did the mantra. *The mantra.*

Tired, but smoothly as silk, I glided into the town of Leh. Nice small touristy town. I was in no mood for a loaf and settled down for the night. The hotel was way above my budget but after the rigours of the two-day ride, I had earned a good night's rest.

Leh has some good eating places. I was sitting in one

of the smaller restaurants, reading a book and waiting for lunch. Some Nepali waiters were abusing the customers, and even the manager, amongst themselves, speaking in their own language. Saying things like, 'The mother-fucker at table four wants some more napkins', 'the pansy manager is checking the store again, the bastard!' and 'There come the misers from yesterday and I am not serving those cunts'. I enjoyed the ribald comments until I heard them call me 'the fatso at table two'. This I did not like at all and had no wish to hear further refinements on my body or my sex life or my lineage. I quickly called one of the waiters and asked him, in Nepali, to get me some water. Their merry conversation died instantly.

Did the usual. Visited the spots and gawked at things. Bought only books. Ladakhi women are pretty modern. They were dressed in the latest outfits and looked good in them, a pleasure to behold. One shopkeeper expressed surprise that I had travelled so far alone. Then began to watch me carefully as I browsed through his handicraft shop. I didn't seem to be making a good impression on people anymore.

The Shanti Stupa overlooks the town from a small hillock. I was going around the place when I saw a foreign couple. They were doing the usual things and visiting different parts of the Stupa and the small monastery nearby. I did not pay them much attention except when the woman slapped the man. They were putting on their shoes when she did this. Since I was the only other person nearby, the woman complained to me. The man proved to be a doped-out junkie who had been following her around all morning. The way he had gathered filth on himself, sex with a woman should have been a distant dream. I dropped her off to town.

Kurum, good old Kurum, was standing outside the new hotel to which I had shifted in the morning. This place was more in my league. Kurum had just got into town, a full two days after me. If I had had a problem on the road, my goose would have been cooked, waiting for Kurum and his party. His mechanic and the driver wished me like old friends. Breakfast on the free lane is a powerful friendship-cementer. I told Kurum I was finished with Leh and would be heading back the next day. See you in Manali, I said.

Then I saw a group of young men who looked familiar because they did *namaste* the traditional way. Turned out they were boys who had worked in my hotel in Gangtok. Neelam, Vinod and Dawa were as astounded to see me as I was to see them. They were on a break and insisted on treating me to momos. The place they took me to was cheap, clean and the food was good. Another lesson for the road is to try and find where the waiters eat in places of tourist interest. They know where to get the best bargain.

Ran into Chris and Samantha again. They hadn't had any more problems on the road. So much for me and my predictions. They treated me to dinner. Some days, the freebies just keep coming.

17

I decided to push my luck and reach Manali, normally a two-day journey, in a day. One for the books, so to speak. The bike had been tanked up. I was not going to pay any other Waldorfs I might encounter on the way any extras. Got up at 4.30 and by 5 a.m. I was on the road. An early morning ride is something else. Headlights on under a starry sky. Gentle cold breeze and a clean road ahead. I made good time in the morning.

The dawn sky turned a gentle orange and the last stars disappeared. I watched the sun come slowly above the horizon. I am not what you would call a sentimental man but I felt raw that day. It was a lonely ride and the immensity of the land bothered me. At seven I had an egg and a couple of soggy slices of bread with a cup of tea at a tiny army outpost.

When you pass human beings on the road there is a lot of smiling, waving of hands, honking of horns and general acknowledgement of each other. As civilization nears, this best behaviour comes back to normal and we start to ignore each other.

I am not ashamed to say that I cried copiously that day. Laughed, too. I lost it for a while there, I am truly happy to say. Something happened that day and I would take that day to my grave.

This was biking paradise. I saw solitary riders on bikes, I saw them in pairs, I saw them in scores and they all waved, smiled, honked and sped away. There were Indians, men and women, and plenty of foreigners. Happy people. For a day at least.

The truckers and the tankers move in pairs. A single truck is a dead truck. They picnic on the way. Bearded ruffians smile, wave, shout and are happy to see you. Driving was courteous in that area.

The best part of the day was when I was offered some butter tea by Dorjee, a yak-herd. I had stopped for a piddle and Dorjee came and started to talk to me even as I was in action. Embarrassing. The more I turned away, the more he rotated with me. When he found out that I was from Sikkim, he turned positively effusive. He had heard about it from his grandfather. A cigarette sealed our friendship and he offered me tea in his tent. (Two hot mugs of rich butter tea and I didn't need to eat till Manali.) These are lonely men, with only their dogs for company. Fierce brutes. The dogs, I mean. One of the brutes kept showing me his huge teeth. I told Dorjee about my crying and he nodded sympathetically. The deities will be pleased with that, he said. I don't know what he meant.

When I passed the Waldorf at Sharchu in the middle of the day I gave the crook the up-yours sign. Don't know if he understood but I felt vindicated. During a particularly rough crossing at a small river, I nearly overturned and could not get my bike upright until help came from the vehicle behind me. Then I got caught in the middle of an army convoy and the dust was so thick my eyes clogged over and I had to stop. My mouth felt like I had bitten into a mud pie. Got stuck in a landslide for an hour. The weather held till a slight shower came, near Manali. It had taken me sixteen hours of hard riding but it had been worth every crazy minute.

18

Back in the cottage, I found it was infested with all sorts of creatures big and small. I had a running battle with a huge rat and she came on top every time. There were a couple of smaller ones I didn't bother with as they showed me respect. The big one bruised my ego by cavorting about openly in my presence. The mice had given birth everywhere and I grew sick of transporting their pink slimy babies outside the house. Night time ushered in rat reggae on the ceiling.

There were a couple of funny-looking lizards which attempted entry to the house, but only formally, through the front door. I construed it was the flies that attracted them and not my personal charm. All the caterpillars, grasshoppers, beetles and other assorted creepy-crawlies in Manali seemed to make a beeline for this cottage—the bees, too. The swarms of flies did nothing to enhance the beauty of my surroundings. The garden outside was wild with bushes that trespassed onto the verandah. A gardener would demand a king's ransom to clean the place. Sometimes, I saw a few village women cutting the grass to take it away. They didn't ask permission but I was glad to see them lighten the shrubbery.

I had yet to get a handle on the social etiquette of the place. 'Common property' seemed to be the rule of thumb. There was a temple nearby, a busy place resounding with the constant beating of drums. Very attractive for a would-be writer in search of silence, I don't think. The catch was that I had already paid a six-month advance rent on the place. The shrewd businessman had got me by the short and curlies. I just had to battle it out with the local fauna and the percussion from next door. With the help of ear-mufflers and some insecticide. And an air rifle, too. And a Rambo knife. I devoted a part of the day to hunting. The best thing about the place was the birdsong in the morning. All types, shapes and sizes of the feathered creatures appeared every day. I didn't shoot them.

Then came a whacking big black monster of a snake. I spotted it from the corner of my eye in the kitchen as it was checking out my provisions. I bounded upstairs to pull on my riding boots, the only protection at hand. Thank you, God, for mobile phones. Feverishly, I called for help and the troops arrived shortly. All the while, I was cowering on top of the stairs, looking to see where the slimy thing was. The damn snake had disappeared, having probably apprehended my call for help. That was that. I was done with the place, advance paid or not.

I went first to Dharamshala, where the Dalai Lama stays, before returning to pack. Kurum, dear old Kurum, the man who tried to give me a group ride but could not, gave me a woman as a pillion rider instead. Sarah, an Israeli in her mid-thirties, and Kurum's friend. Since it was to be a three-day sojourn, I didn't carry much luggage and Sarah had even less. We started early and the rain soon joined us. Two hours into the ride and we were both soaking wet. I could not put on my rain gear as Sarah had none. My offer to her to use my raincoat was rejected so we decided to go wet. There was a very heavy downpour at one stretch and we took refuge in a cowshed. The woman was blue and shivering uncontrollably. I gave her my jacket, and my raincoat, which, this time, was quietly accepted. Pretty woman, with mascara-laced cheeks. A student of Buddhism and based in Dharamshala, Mcleodganj. No wonder she had hardly any luggage.

Our halt overnight was at a place called Bir. Lovely village in the Himachal hills. Gentle, rolling slopes on which paragliding holds sway over all other activity. We camped in the Tibetan colony there. Blue Sarah and me. The fried rice was great.

After a refreshing night, Sarah regained her original complexion. White Sarah and me, we left for Mcleodganj. What a lovely town! Despite the drizzle the place got to me instantly. Sarah planted a full-blown kiss on my lips and disappeared into the arms of her boyfriend.

Mcleodganj had a peaceful atmosphere, but was at the same time vibrant and colourful. Hard-working Tibetans did brisk business with the tourists. Plenty of foreigners, supporters of the Tibetan cause, thronged the town. The owner of a bookshop was a well-read Tibetan poet who had written an appeal denouncing the Beijing Games. He handed me a flier and a diatribe. Poor chap! I could see the fire in his impotent eyes. The Tibetan bread *phalay*, and the butter tea reminded me of home. Tried half-heartedly to get a glimpse of the great Lama, knowing it was nigh impossible.

Lhakpa, of a small restaurant, became a friend. He played a guitar all day. He must have been new at it because he was the worst I'd heard in a long time. I taught him a few songs and he gave me a few cups of tea in lieu of tuition fees. Lhakpa was waiting to go abroad, every young Tibetan's dream. Hope he finds his way in the world because China's not going away.

It was one long, lousy ride back to Manali. Broke the news of my leaving to the owner. He was very kind about it, in words. I waited for signs of an offer of a refund. High hopes. He seemed to think he had done me a big favour, not having asked for the whole year's rent in the first place. Hopes dashed, and wincing with financial pain, I found solace in packing with zeal. A couple of extra bags were sent by road to Delhi and the rest would go on the bike.

I had my first proper toss on the bike. Slow motion. I was driving at ten kilometres an hour and it was a slow skid on a small turn leading to the centre of Manali. I fell on top of a stone wall slowly, and barely scratched my hand. The bike spilled oil and I realized I'd damaged the gears. The price of not using the bars, those guards in front of the bike which protect the rider's legs, and the side of the bikes from damage. Only sissies use it. Or wise guys.

Hauled the leaking machine to a grim garage-owner and mechanic who looked like he hadn't had sex for ages. Good and silent man to watch when he was working. Not a very pretty sight when not working. Gruff grunts were all he grudgingly let out. He cuffed his handymen regularly over the ears. Liked to talk with his hands, the miserable bugger.

A day later I was back with the exact same problem, having skidded on a bridge near town. I hadn't fallen down this time but the bike had been damaged again. Django couldn't believe his eyes. Words, already a trickle for him, died completely. With a shake of his head he waded into his work. Being looked down on by a sex-starved mechanic felt horrible.

I didn't know what caused the two accidents in a row, because I'd been riding slow on both occasions. All this delayed my departure from Manali, and Django looked disappointed. Maybe I was fated to stay a few days extra to pay my dues to the local deities. There was this Tibetan woman who rode an Enfield. Seeing a lady riding this monster turned me on. Then I saw two white women on bikes. Double turn-on. That was perhaps why I fell.

One of the final sights of the town was of a young hippie, completely in his own world, lying sprawled outside a shop. Mouth open, eyes vacant and dribble on his chin. The shopkeeper didn't appear to be bothered and neither were passers-by. The same fellow got to his feet suddenly and stared vacantly into another shop, and nobody cared. Manali was shockproof.

Goodbyes all around. Grandpop-of-the-shop fame and the doggy eyes, viewed my departure as a personal betrayal. Like I'd knocked up his daughter and then neglected to marry her. My other friends gave me a normal farewell, Manali-style. Booze. Chilli chicken. Booze. Fried chicken. Booze. Chicken tikka. Booze. Chicken kebab.

In a way I'd enjoyed the lively place, but we were not to have a long affair. Just a passing fling.

19

It was the longest ride so far. Eighteen hours on the road from Manali to Delhi. I don't know which parts of Punjab I passed through because I was trying out a new route and got a little lost. Saw two inebriated Sardars on the road and asked them for directions. They asked me my family history. They were drunk in the middle of the afternoon and overflowing with the milk of human kindness, having drunk plenty of buffalo milk in their youth and a good bit of barley milk that day. After pointing me in the right direction they offered me help in any other way. This was a small panchayat road and their van and my bike had blocked the road. A tractor going my way honked and my two heroes rushed up to its driver hurling the kind of colourful imprecations heard only in Punjab. I took off.

The first puncture of the journey took place in Mehsana, somewhere between Chandigarh and Delhi. Around 7.30 in the evening the telltale wobble set in and

I 'Oh-shitted'. Already dark, this was bad timing. I hobbled along till I came to some lights. On inquiry, I was informed that the nearest repair shop was a kilometre away. No way was I going to be able make it that far with a flat. I saw an air pump in the dimly lit teashop nearby. Suresh, the vendor, took pity on me and got to work with a vengeance with the pump, and the entire gang of tea-drinkers pitched in. Some hauled out the luggage, others tilted the bike, still others brought me black tea, and I was not allowed to lift a finger. They just wanted to hear my story. I gave them a juiced-up version. I bought everyone a round of tea and some *matri*, a local biscuit. An autorickshaw-driver, a smart alec, invited me for a drink of the local brew. Cigarettes to anyone who cared to smoke and I was among friends. I'd found in the course of my personal odyssey that smokes are an effective way of breaking the ice anywhere, but I was stunned, nevertheless, by the courtesy shown to me by these rural folk of Haryana. To top it all, Suresh charged me only for the tea and the biscuits. Not being allowed to pay him for his labour, I could only leave him what I hoped was an adequate tip.

Thus far, I had ridden the east coast, and then taken the east-to-west route from Sikkim to Leh, in Kashmir. Now I intended to hit the cow belt through Uttar Pradesh and

Bihar. Ramesh, my brother-in-law, is also somewhat affected by wanderlust, but he suffered, too, from the city sickness of having no time to do his stuff. This time he was fated to do the boogie with me and we made plans to make it together to his hometown, Varanasi, in two days. The day we set out was hot, dry and dusty. We stopped in the middle of nowhere to have lunch. The owner of the eatery was a toughie called Surendra, gleaming in a starched white kurta. He was all smiles in his new role as an hotelier but the look in his eyes told me he still had to iron out some old bad habits, such as his propensity to beat up people who made him uncomfortable. Five or six of his clones in white were hanging around, a bunch of goondas smiling pleasantly but clearly oozing testosterone. Ramesh looks like the actor Nana Patekar who also looks like a toughie. He was in his element with the UP-style mafia regarding us curiously. Ramesh let out, ever so casually, that I was in the IAS, and that aroused their interest considerably. Six pairs of beady eyes fixed on us with suspicion. We were pulling a fast one on them. How could a service officer be on a motorcycle? In these parts of the country the service I belonged to is so far removed from the people that its officials are slotted with the superstars. You don't find a Sunjay Dutt with Nana Patekar as his pillion in your hotel. Then I contributed my own airy numbers, dropping names of batchmates they'd recognize. Their attitude swiftly underwent a metamorphosis. The watchful faces lit up with sycophantic fervour. I deemed it time for us to move.

After twelve hours of riding we'd made it only as far as Bareilly. Ramesh tried to take over the bars, but I cut his attempt short. You don't fool with the traffic in the highways, so he was relegated to sit as pillion for the rest of the journey. He had to go back to his wife and kid in one piece, and I still had a lot of road to cover. I was not taking chances.

The hotel in Bareilly felt like an airport, complete with Customs Clearance at the reception. Along with Homeland Security. That may have had something to do with the fact that both Ramesh and I are bearded individuals. The clerk asked Ramesh for his ID, which was promptly shown. I was busy with the luggage so I escaped the interrogation. Then I was asked to fill in my particulars, an unusual procedure in such parts. We'd barely settled in our room when we were accosted by Homeland Security once again. It was my ID the man wanted to see this time. Amused; I handed over my driving licence. Satisfied, he politely left—only to return to ask again for my ID to show to his superiors downstairs. Ramesh blew his top and I added my bit. 'Mother-fuckers', 'sister-fuckers', 'sons of whores', 'pricks', 'assholes', the works—everything but the ID—is what they got from us. Homeland Security backed off quickly. We were left in peace and quiet after that. What was that all about? Never quite understood.

There is this strange contraption commonly to be observed on the roads in western UP. It is called 'jugar', which literally means 'arrangement'. Diesel pumps for drawing water are put on a locally made chassis and, voila, you have a vehicle that can be used to ferry people. Nasty piece of work, spewing noxious fumes, driven by unlicensed characters and without any registration. A menace to all, but it works! The ingenuity of Indians is remarkable—as is the impunity with which our laws may be flouted.

Another horrible day. Began to rain early in the morning. We heard on the news that there was a major depression over the Bay of Bengal and storms were pounding the eastern and northern parts of India. Small consolation, knowing that. To cap our misery we had a flat tyre. The second in quick succession. I didn't like this habit the bike appeared to be developing. Fortunately, it took place right in front of a repair shop, and in a way, we were glad for a respite from the rain.

Huddled under a small piece of tarpaulin we smoked greedily. Viewing the back of the workman with deep suspicion, I wondered, how could the puncture occur at a place so convenient to him? Was the bastard scattering nails on the road? Suspicious, very, very suspicious.

A fourteen-hour ride after that, and Ramesh began showing signs of cracking up. I didn't blame him. Riding pillion for long hours is very uncomfortable. Add daddy-long-legs and you could gauge his misery. Every time we stopped for a tea break, it took longer to get back on the road. Initially it was one cigarette per break. Then my man upped that to two, and then three. He owned up like the man he was and confided that his bones had projected from his body and joined the structure of the bike—or so it seemed to him. On one of our frequent stops we met a young man who latched on to Ramesh, discovered that he used to work with an English-language TV channel, and asked for help with a reporting job on the sister Hindi channel. The fellow was a jeweller in a mofussil town. God knew the reason for his request. People ask too many questions on the road and Ramesh does not lie. A few more days with me and I would set him right. The long road was for liars. That was the only way to survive on it.

There was a severe storm and trees lay uprooted along the wayside. Traffic was stopped at various places but the local people were like locusts on the trees. Within no time the way would be cleared with dozens of locals hacking at the trunks for firewood. We saw a giant tree in the act of falling down on the road just twenty feet away. Scary.

India were in the finals of the shortest version of cricket. Ramesh and I were desperate to catch the play on TV, but no hotel rooms were available in any of the small towns we passed. Jagdishpur was a slightly bigger place but no hotel room offered television. With the finals getting out of reach, we puttered miserably into Sultanpur, wet, cold and hungry. Near the bus station we finally found a room with television and watched the final few overs. India won and we celebrated by dropping off to sleep on our big double bed. This was all that Sultanpur had to offer us, a double bed in a dirty hotel near the bus station, with no food. The person at the reception was a perpetual grinner. The rictus grew wider every time he had to answer in the negative. Do you have another room? No! Big smile. Do you have food? No! Even bigger smile. Do you have mineral water? No! Alfred E. Neuman smile. Do you have another blanket? No! No! No! And he was rolling in mirth.

The next day was my turn to look happy. I fingered a hundred-rupee note in his face, put it in my pocket, gave him a huge smile, and scooted. No tip. Cheap but satisfying revenge.

It took us three days to get to Varanasi. Raining as usual. Ramesh and I were one soggy mess. Despite the discomfort, he was slow to complain. The strong, silent type. Taking things on the chin. We stopped for a roadside breakfast and ate freshly cooked potato patties. Standing space only. We gobbled down more than our usual intake of food. A tika-wearing, pot-bellied, middle-aged man stood in the rain two feet away and gawked openly, the holy ash on his forehead slowly dripping down his face.

One expects chaotic traffic in many of India's older towns, but the situation in Varanasi was completely mad. Even bikes were forced to slow down. Inches separated you from the next vehicle. The daddy-long-legs touched everything we passed, fetching their owner reproachful glances from all sides. But Ramesh didn't care, only taking a vow in the holy city of Varanasi that he would never again ride a bike for longer than the shortest journey. Destination arrived at, he got off the machine with alacrity.

Ramesh's parents are solid people. The old man is a Gandhian and has lived his life by those standards. Ramesh's mother is into prayers. Varanasi does that to you. Nice, healthy vegetarian fare was provided to us world-weary travellers.

We went for a ride on the river, but not before some serious haggling with the boatmen. The Ganga at night, with the ghats as a backdrop, is eerily beautiful. We had some peanuts and some rum. One of the older boatmen was already drunk but sidled up to us hoping for a shot of our rum. He got peanuts instead. The burning ghats were a sad sight, but the others looked festive, what with the lights and the people and the pujas they engaged in. The city is full of priests, pimps, pushers and pilgrims, a confluence of contradictions. Old yet modern. Abounding in holy men and prostitutes. Carrying on a vibrant life alongside a constant stream of dead bodies. Prayers and drugs. Hindustanis and hippies. Varanasi rocks!

Dilip, the head boatman who'd ferried us, was a goldmine of information, with a smattering of English thrown in for good measure. He had obviously learnt the language while swindling foreigners into paying a bomb for a boat ride. He informed us that five types of Hindus are not cremated on the ghats and that their bodies were released to the river. These included sadhus, those dead of snakebite, unmarried pregnant women, people with leprosy and other contagious diseases, and children below ten years of age.

Dilip tried to con us into taking a longer ride with him the next day. When Ramesh was busy talking to the other boatmen, Dilip offered me a woman, for a price of course. My long, unkempt hair and beard must have caused me to look starved of both civilization and sex.

Ramesh was to fly back after a few days in Varanasi. I was tempted to stay. I felt a sense of comfort, a feeling of having been there before—although this was my first visit, at least in this life.

Around eleven one morning, when I was finally comfortable with the idea of moving on, I promised myself another, longer visit to the place. The Gandhian, I suspected, had regarded my antics with some concern for my sanity. A couple of times, I caught him looking at me and shaking his head. There followed a long discussion about the route I should take to Jharkhand state. I said my goodbyes, apologized for the state of Ramesh's ass, and moved on with my life. Such as it was.

20

Started relatively late. I kept having to stop and ask for directions. Each time, a crowd of curious onlookers gathered to listen in on the proceedings. After hearing my chaste Hindi, they lost interest. All except the die-hard variety, the wise guys of the road, who made nasty comments, asked probing questions and generally looked for a laugh. I took it easy. This was not the nicest part of the country; I could get into trouble. There wasn't a policeman I could turn to for miles around. Finally, I met someone on a motorcycle who seemed a decent chap. He led me to the right bifurcation and showed me the straight road from there on. Some words of advice were also thrown in: don't give anybody a ride; don't talk to anybody in teashops; don't react to comments flung at you; don't tell anybody where you are going; don't show anybody your money; don't move in the dark if you can help it. Above all, don't ask any old bloke for directions.

Crossed over the border from eastern UP to Jharkhand. The ride on the plateau was lovely, till I got smacked once again by a thunderstorm. It rained all the way to Sadbharva. The storm darkened the skies so heavily, I had to switch on my headlights. The heavy rain and poor visibility forced me to stop under a tree and even there, I continued to be drenched. This was a backward region of the country and I knew that hotels would be nowhere to be found. I had to push on anxiously, the lightning doing nothing to alleviate my terror. Great cracking wallops were rollicking on the plains. Rivulets formed on the road and at times I had to wade through calf-high water.

The town of Daltonganj appeared in the soaking rain and the night. Was tempted to halt there but my missionary cousin was waiting just an hour away. Stopped to buy some brandy at a bar. I had leaned the bike on the side-stand and when I came back I saw it lying on the ground. The ground had grown so soggy in the rain, the stand had sunk clean inside it. With the help of a passing gentleman, I righted the bike and continued for another hour of a nightmarish ride. Numb from the cold and the bumping over potholes, I spotted cousin dear through the gloom. Standing in the pouring rain on the main road in a place where electricity had yet to find its way. The Navjeevan Hospital complex, in which my cousin lived and worked, at least had a generator and a warm bed.

Chering Choden Tenzing has devoted her life to God's work. Jesus called and she answered. Seven years running in the boondocks, and she is happy. The light of a missionary shines in her eyes. The same eyes which have looked at me with love—and, not infrequently, with disdain and pity for not seeing the light. She is the youngest of four sisters and a brother, and is a first cousin of mine. A decade younger than me, she laid down the law for me, the black sheep, anyway. No drinking and no smoking on the premises of the hospital. Well, you know me by now. I fished out a cigarette and poured myself a glass of brandy. Not in her presence of course. One does not mess with people who have a hotline to God.

Now for a bit of personal history (that you were probably dying to hear). Half my family are Christians and half Buddhists. Every generation mutates this way. Somehow, it is usually the eldest who turns to Christianity while the younger brothers gravitate to Buddhism, the religion their wives usually follow. My generation onwards, a hardening of positions has taken place. My grandfather was a pastor and an evangelist. So Chering treats me as the one in the fold who got lost, and hopes for my return. Me, of the meditation and the Sanskrit prayers and the diamond practice. I say, do your thing and do it well. My cousin has done just that. A doctor by profession, she is doing sterling work with her team gladly in this godforsaken place. No, not a godforsaken place, because God is here and working his magic.

The next day was educative. I was sent out with an extension officer of a serious temperament. He on his bike, and me on mine through slushy village footpaths. It had to be a pathetic life for the tribals living here. Outdoor patients ravaged by tuberculosis formed the bulk of the population. A grown man, weighing only twenty-five kilograms, had to be supported by the officer all the way to his check-up at Navjivan. The chap was skin and bones. The biggest thing about him seemed to be his kneecaps. Another patient was being persuaded to revisit the hospital. With a jolt I realized it was for me to carry the bacteria-infested bloke to the treatment centre. I cringed inside— and then was assailed by shame for feeling that way. I recognized that I had to learn to do more than spout prayers if I wanted to aspire to human decency. When the poor wretch promised to return for treatment to the clinic the next day, I felt vindicated. I suspected this was one of Chering's ploys to torture the lost sheep. To get even, I drank and smoked with gusto in her hallowed premises.

These people live simple lives and their dedication is phenomenal. I guess a higher calling does that to you. When you work for others you work with a mission. There is only the slight danger of arrogance at the idea of doing more good than others.

The food in the common canteen was nourishing and simply orchestrated, with potato as the leading member of the choir. Chering put me up in the guest house, actually just a spare room that had been hurriedly cleaned. She lives in a simple two-room cottage by herself, and eats in the canteen. I met her colleagues over meals. They were doctors, doing work they were actually supposed to do. Curing the poorest of the poor.

21

I have this friend, Mridula, a colleague in the service, posted in Ranchi, the capital of Jharkhand state. I don't meet her often, which is a euphemistic statement because we meet only once in a decade, or so it seems. We'd last met in 1997, when she had helped me conduct some rites for my late father at Bodhgaya. The same year, she and her husband Shivendu, another service officer, were my guests in Gangtok. Then we lost touch. The last I'd heard of them they were in the States.

Just about the time I was leaving Manali, I got this call from Mridula. She was back in Ranchi. I jumped at the chance to meet her as Ranchi featured on that leg of my trip. The fates must have conspired, because she kindly invited me to stay with her and her family. Good food and a clean bed have gone up in my list of priorities. Somewhat near the top, in fact, so I accepted with eagerness.

It was an uneventful ride to Ranchi. Upon entry I

managed as usual to find the general location and stopped for more precise directions. My bad luck lay in asking a near-deaf rickshawallah. What with the roar of the bike, and the traffic, our exchange turned into something like a bad dream. A Good Samaritan stopped and asked me where I wanted to go. I told him the address, he knew the house, and he also wanted to know what business I had there. This cheesed me off and I told him to mind his own business. He smiled and said Mridula had been in his class in college, and I hurriedly pulled on a smile and told him she'd been my batchmate. Samaritan Subramanian and I kept smiling as he led me to Mridula's house.

Mridula was shocked at my appearance. I could tell by her rounded eyes. The bureaucrat in her refused to accept such a dramatic change in her friend. A change for the worse. After I cleaned up, she looked a bit relieved, and any regret she may have felt about inviting a tramp home seemed to abate. Cecilia remembered me and my dogs. She was Mridula's lady Jeeves and had accompanied her to Sikkim a decade ago. My dogs and me, we meant the same to Cecilia. (*Cecilia, you're breaking my heart!*)

I was taken to meet other old colleagues. Satpathy was holding court in his office like the seasoned bureaucrat he had become. With a preoccupied look he leaped to his feet and welcomed me with outstretched arms as the captain of the recently victorious Indian cricket team. 'Mr Dhoni, welcome!' The win was on everybody's mind, the young captain was a boy from Ranchi, my hair was wet, long and slicked back in the captain's style and I suppose

I looked fitter and leaner than Satpathy remembered me to be. When he realized it was old Tenzing standing there, the embarrassment was palpable.

But the seasoned bureaucrat that he is, it took him less than a minute to recover. And we were off to the past. Munigala, another colleague, could not remember me. The amnesia was mutual. But we shook hands like old brothers-in-arms and he told me the story of his life, although I hadn't asked him to.

I know that there is a divide between the honest and dishonest officers in all the states. The honest ones are losing the battle on a daily basis. Some stay and fight every single day. Others look away and manage to keep their own noses clean. Some are looking for a way of moving out of the system somehow. I met a lot of bureaucrats in the state, mainly because of Mridula. In the other states I avoided meeting them as a rule.

A senior officer lamented that the socialist system of governance was at the bottom of the present ills in the bureaucracy. Policy-makers were doing only the routine job of governance and those who had to implement the policies had surrendered all power to the politicians.

There is a serious lack of policy-makers in this country, a paucity of long-term thinking, and of think-tanks. To give an example, take the department of transport. The minister and the Secretary should be putting their heads together to find long-term solutions to transport problems in a state. Instead, the minister shows active interest in the transfers of personnel in his department—with the connivance of the Secretary—a job better undertaken by the transport commissioner's office. This weakens the commissioner's position, he loses control over his subordinates, and so on, and on, the problem goes. And somehow, the country stumbles along.

The motorcycle was in need of some repairs. The clutch, the indicators, headlights, self-starter, the tubes in the tyre, loosened screws everywhere, etc. A man came and collected the bike and I handed him the list of jobs to be done, and the money. The perks of the bureaucracy for a day again.

Lunch was at the house of Rajbala and Jyothi, a couple in the service. Good south Indian food, after what seemed like ages, in the heart of the tribal belt of north India. I should know how good it really was. I have lived a lifetime down south.

Aggarwal had been the chap who'd speeded up freeing me of my shackles in Kerala. He'd processed and signed much of the paperwork required when leaving the service, and I was let go quickly and efficiently on his personal initiative. He was now based in Ranchi, his hometown. I was fond of him and we'd spent many a happy hour together. He used to enjoy my cheap jokes and I like people who enjoy my cheap jokes. A happy combination. He comes from a business family and he made it on his own steam into the service without the active support of anyone at home. We met at Mridula's for dinner.

The stint in Ranchi was a round of meals in different houses. Subramanian called me over for a nice Andhra breakfast. So engrossed was he in talking, and his entire family in listening, that even by eleven the breakfast had not been served. I wondered if I'd imagined the invitation and sheepishly asked if there was anything going. And then it was food all the way.

Satpathy gave me lunch and I was interviewed by Manoj of the *Indian Express* in Ranchi. The next day the story of my expedition was flashed all around the country and phone calls started pouring in. Didn't know whether to thank him or kick his ass.

Mr Sahni is a fascinating Sardarji in his sixties who has the energy of someone half his age, and the ideals of a twenty-year-old. His passion is the Rotary Club and its activities. He is busy sending out and bringing in exchange students. I'd first met him in Gangtok at my hotel, where he had brought a group of young Americans and I was singing for the band in the evening.

With some people you hit it off, just like that. We swung into our friendship, like kids. Now I was at his doorstep and the swinging kicked in early. The man has got a house filled with the choicest wines from all over the world. Gifts from his students. We attacked a couple of bottles with gusto. Mrs Sahni is an erudite lady and a splendid hostess. Shantanu, their twenty-year-old adopted son, is from the Munda tribe. He is in touch with his biological parents and he is not a Sikh. Not yet, anyway. With a father like that I would have become a Sikh like a shot.

Mr Sahni was the one to send my daughter to Alaska. There were exchange students in Ranchi and I went to meet some of them just to see what my daughter would be doing in Alaska in the Rotary programme. I saw young girls and boys giving small presentations about their countries. I saw the Rotary way of doing things. Impressive. And I danced with sheer joy at the opportunity afforded to my daughter. I rocked for an hour. Others were dancing too. The late 1970s and early '80s dancing numbers were on, and my feet moved like they hadn't in two decades. I found my dancing form in Ranchi. Something I'd thought I'd lost forever, when I became a stuffed frog in the IAS. There were some hot women in the Rotary group that evening. A decided bonus.

Aggarwal gave me a meal in his house early next morning. I had wished my hostess goodbye with the hope of meetings in the future that would occur more frequently than once in ten years. We wound things up with a photo session.

I was supposed to go to a non-governmental organization somewhere north of Ranchi which was said to be doing great work for women and children. Phone calls were made and contacts established. On the way I saw a signpost reading 'Barhi'. This was a place I had never visited but one whose name I'd seen on similar signposts all my life, when travelling between Gangtok in Sikkim and Siliguri in West Bengal. Freedom. I changed course and headed for Barhi. Lunch was at a place with a singing waiter. There were no other customers so he concentrated on shattering my eardrums. He was the type of singer who looked deep into your eyes, probing for signs of adulation. The lousy food and the horrible accompaniment was a lethal combination. I think even the machine felt it, weeping oil copiously as it did when I walked back to it after lunch.

Worried about the trail of oil behind me, I knew I needed a mechanic, and fast. The town of Jhumri Tilaya was my next halt. It is a huddle of houses on both sides of the road. A very small place, for one so well known to most Indians of my generation because it frequently featured in Hindi movie dialogues of the 1970s and '80s. I stopped at the first mechanic's I saw and he pointed me to the Enfield specialist across the road. I surrendered my bike to my first choice anyway. He gave me a stool and a cup of tea. He also gave me a lesson in life.

Guddu, the mechanic, was Muslim. He was a superb mechanic who kept me entertained with stories while working on the bike. Spare parts were not available but those vacancies he filled in with parts from other makes, with at least a year's guarantee. Guddu said he came from a family of mechanics, and passed down some folklore about his father doing work for some foreigners two decades ago, and such like. I surmised I would be part of some equally exciting story in the future. A big and friendly crowd gathered to watch the proceedings. Guddu said 'good work and good behaviour' needed to go together. I agreed and paid him a paltry hundred bucks. Till then, I had the good fortune to have met only decent mechanics, men who were good at their jobs and who didn't overcharge me, if they charged me at all. Doubtless, some bastard would be waiting around the corner to screw me, and my cosmic network told me I would meet him soon.

From Jharkhand, instead of heading towards Chhattisgarh state, I wound my way into Bihar. The roads had been so spectacularly bad, I'd covered less than 300 kilometres when night fell. By popular disrepute, this was not a place for night riding if you knew what was good for you, so I halted at the first town I arrived in, Bihar Sharief. Small, dusty joint. The best bet for the night is a hotel with some sort of parking and a padlocked gate. I was expecting problems but people turned out to be extremely helpful and courteous on the road. Then, there was this waiter. Very efficient, with a gung-ho attitude. 'Can do' was his motto. He did his best. Cleaned the room once again, changed the bedsheets but was defeated when I asked for a fresh towel. So we compromised on a half-damp rag, but at least I knew that it had been washed. There was an all-pervasive smell of urine in the room. I found it so intolerable that I got up in the night and peed in a corner of the room. Marking my territory, so to speak.

Started early. The overpowering stench saw to that. I had something to eat at a place called 'ENGLISH'. The old man at the dhaba was a well-informed bloke. He regaled me with stories about the area. He knew about Sikkim and the merger. He informed me about the animal-traders from Sikkim and Tibet who used to come to the famous Sonepur fair in the heady days of his youth. There is a type of horse which is still called 'Bhotay' and is still bred in this part of the country. Bhotay means 'from Tibet'.

Floods had devastated vast tracts of the land and populations of entire villages were on the road, which has been built to surmount flood-level waters. Buffaloes, cows, goats, chickens, children, women and men and their household possessions on the road, stretching for miles on end. It was one sorry sight. Crawling through the lines, I asked a few villagers whether they had received any help from the government and everywhere the answer was in the negative.

It was a hot day and I saw a few hundred buffaloes lying down in the floodwaters to cool off. Each was masticating with eyes shut tight and wearing an expression bordering on the orgiastic. The poor brutes find the little fun they can.

In a small town further up, I was flagged down rudely by a pig of a policeman at an outpost. I lit into him even before he could ask for a bribe to let me through, which is what I was sure he intended to do. You know how much my small victories over officialdom mean to me. They are, after all, a raised flag—however tiny and ragged— for the helpless and the downtrodden. I got to work on him with a fury I rarely display on the streets. These rats eventually sniff out people who are not afraid of them and, maybe, wield a little authority themselves. The rat's ten colleagues kept a respectful distance, even when I grabbed his collar. By the time I had concluded our little altercation, the man had fished out his rusty, old rifle and even given me a butt salute. A crowd had gathered at the opposite side of the street in pin-drop silence, and when I turned towards them there was a perceptible movement away from me. I felt like a hero in a spaghetti Western movie. Some boys never grow up.

At an accident site near Purnea town, hundreds of people had gathered on the national highway. They had burnt a truck that had mowed down three pedestrians, and were throwing rocks at the policemen on duty. India at work. I quietly slipped away.

Two other sights on that stretch stayed etched in my mind. One was the lines of bare, shitting asses all along the highway, like guns pointed at me. What with the floodwaters raging below them, there was nowhere else for these poor people to go. The other was the scores of dogs run over by trucks on the road, both in Bihar and Bengal.

I stopped for the night at Bagdogra, near Siliguri, only 120 kilometres away from home.

22

I have a rare, dear group of friends in Sikkim, and this time I got to spend a little longer time in their company. The president of the group and the one who holds the key to our activities is Nidup, whose facial expression is one of perpetual surprise. Smiling and helpful always, he is mortally afraid of his wife, a teacher. Despite the fear factor, he keeps pushing the limits of his relationship with Annette. Gambling is his forte. On ludo, dice, cards, billiards, cricket, football and, of course, the king of games, mahjong. All this accompanied by copious quantities of beer. When he's not gambling, he's a family man to the core. He holds an executive position in one of the public sector units.

Agya Sonam, the granddaddy of the group, is an engineer with the state government. Sober, kind and wise—when he isn't drunk. He has a quick wit and enjoys eating huge quantities of meat. Dirty jokes emerge from him in a stream, and he's quick to see the funny side of things. Generous and deeply religious, he, too, lives in fear of his wife. He coos to her on the phone and gets hell from the rest of us for his efforts. His greatest weakness is his daughter.

Jigme Tonyot has handled his in-laws so adroitly, he has almost set up camp in their house. He wins a lot in gambling, and presto, another modern gadget for the home. He knows what he wants and he knows how to get it. Wife, house, a second house, cars and electronic gadgets. He is an outstanding host and, after a decade of marriage, still in love with his wife.

And that brings me to the only bachelor around. Mackey is ego personified, and ego sometimes gets in the way of love. It is our dream to see him married. Different women have been introduced to him and all have been rejected. Sometimes for frivolous reasons like the wrong length of fingernails. He is looking for a woman who does not exist, but he has not given up hope. Pushing forty, but ever optimistic. He's the one who pointed out to us that we were all terrified of the women we'd married. He is our marriage consultant. After a few beers he lectures to his rapt audience with complete conviction about how he thinks conjugal life should be conducted—his theories encompassing severe, if necessary physical disciplining of the female partner. No wonder he isn't married. But I suspect that this is all talk and that he will one day be like putty in the hands of his elusive wife. You should see how afraid he is of his mother and his many sisters.

He told me he'd heard about a girl in Salugarah, a

small town in Bengal a few hours away from Gangtok. In the heat we went, all dressed up, in search of his maiden. His younger brother, who was with us, pointed her out to us, selling lottery tickets on the street. There was a lot of discussion on whether she was the right kind for Mackey. We sipped beer in her father's hotel. Mackey refused to come out of the car, preferring to sweat inside. Since Romeo refused to show himself, or to comment on the girl, we headed back. As we re-entered Sikkim, he announced one more grand rejection. How could he marry a lottery ticket-seller?

Mackey would have done well as an advisor to President Bush. He does not speak much when he's sober, but when he does speak, it's with total conviction. He is a conservative, God-fearing man who does not care where his facts come from or whether logic is on his side. Ideal for the Bush way of doing things.

On the flipside, he is a good friend, always ready to lend a hand, and I like to think he'd take a bullet for me— provided he was drunk enough.

Finally, there is Mishra. A ladies' man to the core, if there ever was one. He does not gamble. He just keeps his shoes polished and his eyes roving. He ties himself in a knot to impress dames anywhere near him. His long-suffering wife knows about this predilection. The carefully groomed hair, the suit perfectly creased over his svelte body, the gleaming footwear, the generous spray of perfume, the fine shave, and the lies, are all dead giveaways—and part of the Mishra magic. The wise woman that his wife is, I think she finds it all quite amusing.

This is the fine company in which I spend many fine hours. We have roaring good times during which gut-splitting laughter is common. I've found my city friends preoccupied, even during party-time. Full-blown enjoyment seemed rare, even cautiously shared. Places like Gangtok, with a slower take on life, and a leisurely pace, yielded limitless fun.

Sikkim, with a population of just over 600,000, is a full-fledged state with all the accompanying paraphernalia. Governor to government-employed gardener. Chief Secretary to stately chowkidars. Too many people catering to too few. There is more than ample time for gossip, even at the top of the heap. I have heard some scurrilous stories myself, involving everyone including the so-and-so lady clerk in such-and-such department who has made disparaging remarks about the man that runs the show. Of course, the man gets to hear about it, and doesn't like it. Ridiculous.

During my stint as a government servant in Sikkim in the mid-1990s, a new team of politicians had just come to power. They called themselves the 'barefoot government'. Rousing slogans for the poor. When I saw the bare feet neatly encased in Gucci shoes, I knew it was time for me to move. There was a Secretary who used to have his car tyres shone with boot polish. There was another who used to show around pictures of his girlfriend during government meetings. Many attended office only as an afterthought, and when they did, it was mainly to drink tea and exchange gossip. I'm not suggesting for a moment that there weren't any hard-working officers with serious purpose—just that those were rare.

In town I met a dear old friend, Dr Rinzing. He is a brilliant doctor whose diagnoses border on the intuitive. Now, after successive promotions, he is a file-pusher in the health department. He was looking bureaucratically depressed. A study of the bureaucracy would reveal a surprising number of clinically depressed people—roughly 25 per cent, I'd say. All of them square pegs hammered into round holes.

23

Karchoong (of the big-head fame) and his two friends were to accompany me to the cold deserts of north Sikkim. Birendra and Lokesh are two talented local guys in the business of shooting and editing films. These three make a good professional combination and have done some work in the documentary line. They have not won any Oscars yet but youth is on their side.

We were to go on two motorcycles and a four-wheel drive, cameras rolling. They told me to meet them at Zero Point, a popular landmark in Gangtok, at 6.30 in the morning. Till seven I was waiting all by myself on the lonely road. Later, I was told, that was because Birendra had had to have a fully satisfying shit. I was to find this a regular occurrence over the three-day trip. Birendra, the camera wizard, was also a full-time shitter. Anytime, anywhere was his motto. He usually chose the most inappropriate time and place to bare his ass. Maybe he should make a documentary on the earth-shattering subject.

Lokesh was the other cool cat. He is an avid biker, like Karchoong, and he falls off the bike at such regular intervals, you can almost time him. Kachoong's new and well-polished bike took a battering under the caring hands of Lokesh the first day. The roads of north Sikkim are always under landslide conditions, with very harsh slopes at times. I didn't blame Lokesh for all his falls. Karchoong, too, was philosophical about Lokesh's effect on his bike.

I was shot, like a movie star, riding this way and that. With the glorious mountains as a backdrop, the waterfalls and the villages. We got to Kabi Lungchok, a site venerated by the Lepcha and Bhutia communities of Sikkim for being the spot where, a few hundred years ago, the two tribes had taken a vow of blood-brotherhood. The stop there had me in full cinematic flow, doing the prayers, and giving a stirring speech for love, unity and so forth. The goddam piece was erased by mistake the same day.

Lunch at my ancestral place, Mangan. My only sibling, Lobsang, has been fighting a losing battle with weight all his life. He has a huge bone structure and a face older than it is. Since our teenage years, he has been mistaken to be my older brother, to his consternation and my delight. He is a conservative man and a damn good son. A quick lunch with him and we were on our way. But not before Karchoong had the local mechanic assess the extent of the Lokesh-effect on his bike.

It was a thrilling ride, part of the excitement arising, of course, from the danger. The road sometimes closely skirted the swirling, icy Teesta. A drop meant certain death. I've seen screaming tourists daring each other down this road. Casualties, mostly fatal, are common, and sometimes the bodies cannot be recovered.

We had tea at a place called Lachen. A small village inhabited by Lachenpas, a Bhutia sub-tribe of mostly yak-owners and shepherds. Nowadays, some of them are into contracts with the government to do a variety of jobs. Rough and tough about sums them up. The lady at the small eatery made some noodles for us. The weather seemed to be acting up and we moved fast on the last leg of the journey. Barring Birendra's toilet breaks. Man, can he shit. He's doglike, leaving his scent everywhere.

Thangu is a one-mule town and the last outpost of civilization on this road. Fourteen thousand feet high, with a few rudimentary hotels and shops. It was cold there. Bitingly cold. As always, we were delayed by some roadwork on the way. The Border Roads Organization, despite the kitschy injunctions that they throw at the public, does a good job keeping the roads open in terrible conditions.

We had needed passes to enter this part of north Sikkim. I had got our passes at Mangan, and shown them for the first time to a drunken cop in Tung, a police outpost in the middle of the jungle where, I'm sure, there isn't much to do but chug a lot. He advised us to make a few copies at Chungthang, the subdivisional headquarters, as the army would need to keep some. The only photocopying machine in Chungthang was inoperable. We decided to take the risk and pressed ahead to Thangu.

The hotel at Thangu was basic, very. My companions fished out their joints and smoked with a frenzy. Cameras rolled, and I was back in form. Then Birendra shat. And the spell was broken. The rooms were so small that our knees touched when we sat on our beds facing each other. In Thangu, at a height of about 14,000 feet, altitude sickness can hit without warning. But we banished that anxiety with laughter, barely edible food and, eventually, exhausted slumber.

For me, sleep was interrupted several times, because it habitually eludes me at high altitudes. Morning finally broke, in a deadly chill. It took me a long time to start up the bike. Huffing and puffing, I managed to fire up the old horse. Found a shop open that had a pair of rock-hard leather gloves on sale. Gleefully, I bought the gloves but could barely move my fingers in them. But a warm, not-so-lively hand is better than a frost-bitten hand—old jungle saying.

We hurtled across the stupefying beauty of the cold desert. The man at the Indian Army checkpost took forever to check our passes. He asked us to park our vehicles in the parking lot, a good distance away. Then we trudged back to the post and he directed us to have tea at the army canteen. He asked us some irrelevant questions and I resented this non-Sikkimese party-pooper for delaying my celebrating my own land. I pulled rank on him, and we were let off.

The last bit to Gurudongmar Lake was really wild, the dirt track a pleasure to ride. Yaks ran away from the alien sound of our motorcycles. Nice, sunny day, without a cloud in the sky. After a steep climb we reached the holy lake at 17,000-plus feet. A marvel. Then, as usual, the crybaby wept. I couldn't help myself. In extenuation, I must tell you that many have felt the same when they reached this spot. Because of the remoteness and the inhospitable terrain, the lake has not been spoilt by the greedy imprint of man. With the snowcapped mountains in the background, the serene and holy lake took my breath away. I shooed everyone away and sat down to talk to it.

After an hour I was ready to face the camera. Yapping and yakking to the box in front of me. The lake had a few more visitors now. A group of travel agents were there to check it out. Most of them were sick and sat listlessly in their vehicles. Only a couple of lucky ones frolicked around, taking photographs. A young and familiar face stared at me. Ginny, a cousin of mine, was part of the visiting group. We whooped and hollered at each other. Well met, sister! A mountain-top meeting.

The ride back was downhill and naturally more rapid. We returned to what is known as civilization. Birendra could not contain his instincts—held in check at the sacred top of the mountain—and shat at the army checkpost. His personal record at above 16,000 feet.

The company had been great and the ride fabulous. These professionals made a nice short film, with music and subtitles. Maybe we'll do a longer one soon.

24

Moving towards the north-eastern states of India, where Assam is the big sister. The chicken-neck to Assam was a long and—need I say it?—wet ride. Passing through the tribal countryside was interesting. Women looked you in the eye boldly. This was a change for me.

Lunch, at a town whose name I don't care to remember, was at—need I say it again?—a dhaba. Usually, at these small eateries all over the India I had traversed, the walls had worn the photographs of the fathers or grandfathers of the present owners. This time, I found the portrait of an Englishman in pride of place. I could not help enquiring why. It transpired that it had been the picture of no Englishman but of the Bengali poet, Michael Madhusudhan Dutt. The dhaba-owner was a fan of Michael, he told me excitedly. It looked like I'd breached a dam and the outpouring started. He went on and on about the poet, his genius, and how he had not received just appreciation from the world, unlike the Nobel-laureate Rabindranath Tagore. He quoted me some lines and chatted some more. I was happy to get back to the rain. I had had enough of Michael to last me for a long time.

Alipurduar is on the Bengal border with Assam. A biggish town, vibrant with colour. I checked into a small hotel as the son of Huein Tsang, the famous Chinese traveller of yore. I had got into the habit of entering the names of famous explorers such as Marco Polo, Fa-Hein, Edmonson, Hillary, Livingstone and others, in hotel registers which sought to know your father's name. Of course, I also fill in my own correct name and home address lest I die in the night. The man at the reception appeared to be from Kerala. He was receptionist, guest relations executive and manager, all rolled into one. I meet Keralites all over the country at the oddest places. I toyed with the idea of shocking the bugger with a volley in his language, but abandoned the thought. I was just too tired to play any more games.

The owner was a sad-looking man who hovered around the counter keeping tabs on his personnel which, at my count, was two. I was to have the pleasure of staying at the same place on my return journey. Two hundred bucks for a decent enough room. Spent my time drying my clothes under the fan and watching a cheap movie on television. Early start the next day, with the sad-looking owner wishing me a fond goodbye. Did this chap ever sleep?

I wanted to go to Arunachal Pradesh, so I took the route to Tezpur. The roads here were being widened as part of a nationwide programme and, at that point, were in a mess. Slushy in the early mornings, turning rapidly dusty as the hours passed. There was a diversion through Sanipeta where the main road had been washed away. Policemen were making money from the taxi operators, all of whom were overloaded. I made it a point of warning all the cabbies going that way. At one checkpost a friendly policeman wanted to chat. He was a Nepali from the Darjeeling hills and we chatted in his language. I was taken aback when he identified my helmet as a Harley Davidson. On the road, surprises never end.

Passed through the town of Rangia. I had come to this town before and stayed a while during the state elections as part of the election commission team. I'd met a young Andhra subdivisional officer full of pep and vinegar. Had to save his neck a couple of times—but what are older bureaucrats for? The funny part was, we used to walk around this huge compound with his fat gunman following us. That was about the only exercise the fellow got. It was hilarious to see the portly status symbol dogging our steps and young Pep-and-Vinegar refusing to let go of his prop even during morning walks. Did he get him to wait outside his bathroom as well?

There had also been this lady Assam civil service officer, buxom and bold, who used to share the local paan with me, flirting outrageously. I remember, too, an excise inspector at whom I'd yelled for some dereliction of duty. The liver patches on his face gave away his department.

Election time is the one time when politicians are on the run and you naturally give them hell, especially as you are not from that state a*nd you represent the Election Commission of India.* Knowing that I would be leaving the service soon and that such raw power would never be in my hands again, I waded into the cringing netas and luckless bureaucrats. Except Old Buxom, of course. I enjoyed myself hugely.

Right now I thought it wise to zip through the town in case anyone I had rubbed the wrong way recognized me. There were many in that category, many unsavoury characters. And a good thrashing was a certainty if I were to be recognized.

The roads were better in this area. I made good time to a small town called Dhekiajuli. An army patrol stopped me for questioning and let me off. Nervous young soldiers along the route fingered their guns. I realized I was in a part of India where all types of outfits are fighting for all types of political causes. From secession to independence to statehood to councils to God-knew-what. The army has special powers, and violence is ever present.

It was already dark and Dhekiajuli seemed the right place to park myself in for the night. The first thing I always looked for was a parking area in which my bike would be safe for the night. Two seedy hotels were rejected because they had no parking facilities. The purported five-star joint in the town turned out to be a train-like construction with a slushy welcome area for guests. But, with a little imagination, you could see it had some sort of a compound and it was not on the main road. The food was fish curry and rice. In Assam, small ponds abound with fish and this is a table staple. Bunked myself in my berth for the night, after eating something like the food you're served on trains.

Managed to reach Tezpur in time to prepare for my next day's assault on Arunachal Pradesh. As luck would have it, there was some sort of strike called for the next day in a district I was to pass through. Decided to give Arunachal a miss and head back to Guwahati the next day. With nothing to do, I ventured on a rickshaw ride around town. Oji Moidunnin Ali gave me a guided tour of the city. We had a long chat about his life, this thin and scrawny man with a lustrous beard, and I. He was very poor but he would not allow his wife to work. The child mortality rate in his house was 50 per cent. Uneducated, and archaic in his beliefs, he personified a large percentage of the population in India. My tip brought tears to his eyes. I left misty-eyed myself, taking with me my Thamzi with this man.

I remember coming here, too, during a period of elections, and meeting a paranoid police officer who was not an Assamese but from a north Indian trading community settled in Assam. He had been ordered to meet me privately with some information. He refused to come inside the hotel I was staying in, claiming that there were politicians in the lobby. So we met in the street, with his eyes darting everywhere. A passer-by happened to merely look at his vehicle, and was endlessly grilled for his pains.

The cop's body language shouted fear. Twitching face and sweat-rimmed upper lip. I nearly burst out laughing. He wouldn't last long, I thought. He was cracking up. Two minutes with me and he scooted, his vehicle carrying a platoon for his protection.

Guwahati was also familiar, my having been sent here for a short period on Government of India duty. The office I'd been sent to had seen some sort of corruption and I was to inquire into the affair. The lazy bums who were responsible came to visit me on the first day in the guest house. They threatened, indirectly, to have the ultras teach me a lesson or two. These fellows had laid a trail a blind man could follow. Things like overwriting on bills, using white ink to conceal things, blatantly breaking procurement rules, the mismatch between samples and the delivered qualities and quantities—the usual. Those guys got fried. I returned to the city occasionally, but not by choice. I used to be put up at the government guest house where I ate the most horrible food that was served there. The city held no charms for me.

I took the scenic ride to Shillong. The colonial British have to be admired for their choice of summer retreats. Shillong still retains it old-world charm but there's too much traffic now. The evening market is a pleasure for sore eyes. Well-dressed, head-turning women shoppers. The roast pork was delicious at the small joint that I ate in. I got talking to the waiter with the grand name of Morning Star. One of the attractive things about people in Meghalaya is that you never know what sort of name will next be sprung at you. From Evening Star, Hopping Stone, General and Captain to Oneboxstar and Cabinet.

I was in for a bit of a bother. I wanted to go to Nagaland, Manipur and Tripura (I had once driven down from Agartala, the capital of Tripura, to Kohima, the capital of Nagaland) but was advised to avoid those states because of the insurgency and related problems there. In Tripura alone, convoys of vehicles had to move with an armed escort in the daytime, eating dust all the way.

I had had occasion to work in Nagaland—on two- or three-day trips—too. I used to sleep in the office because it was safer to do so. Shops closed early. And it grew dark fast. I was working in an office of the ministry of home, and inside the compound, a church was being built. Despite complaints to all and sundry, nothing came of it then. The church must be in full swing now. I'm told the taxes from various underground groups have become a fact of life and the people are resigned to it. These are a brave and straightforward people. They deserve peace.

This time, I chose safety and slunk away early the next morning. In the absence of rain I was whitewashed with dust. The same hotel at Alipurduar. They welcomed me back effusively and even gave me the same room, as if there was something special about it.

The army and the police were everywhere in Assam. Checkpost after checkpost. The army men looked cocky and the policemen demoralized. Outside every army camp, there was a profusion of roadblocks and artificially created humps. Too many to make sense. The mentality of overkill.

In the smaller roadside cafés you get only strong beer. And cheesy waiters serving it. Along the way men fished in their small ponds. For sale and also for the evening meal. Once, a drunkard pointed me in the wrong direction to Alipurduar, but he was quickly corrected by the others. They proceeded to berate him, and I added my bit, threatening to shoot him.

On my way again, I kept to the American side of the road, to avoid the potholes. Another problem was being stopped by gangs of youth for donations for various pujas. The boys are extortionists, really, who put up barricades on the roads and grin at you while declaring the amount they think you should pay. I drove through all of them. I did so nearly over my dead body.

Hawkeye Joe, the observant proprietor of the hotel in Alipurduar, was waiting to pocket the money early in the morning. He looked so sad to see me go. I doubt whether I will ever see him or his town again. That was the end of my very comprehensive tour of the north-east, one bolstered more by memory than movement.

25

Today, I hoped to cross West Bengal and stay somewhere in Bihar. An Indian-style squat toilet is hard on us westernized crappers. I was sorely tested in the morning, so I needed my cup of tea, as openers, pronto. Only problem was there were no teashops open. After two hours on the road, I finally found one just as it was about to open and waited with the owner for the large kettle to come to boil. The shop was a mere shanty, but it had 'cookies', a local species of baked sweet rounds of flour. I ate six of them and the tea man looked nervous, wondering if I'd pay for them all. It was a self-help shop. You dipped your hand in the jar, cocked your eyebrow at the man and when he wiggled his, you took out a cookie. Six times in a row was a new one for him and he was out of his depth. He stopped wiggling his eyebrows and was just goggling at me, moving defensively in front of the jar. I wanted the seventh but decided against it, lest blood be spilt. I paid up, sending the sunshine back to his face, and sped off. The last time I looked behind me, he was back to wiggling his frozen eyebrows.

I had chosen another way back to Siliguri, although the state of the roads hardly differed. Then on to Kishanganj, and Bhagalpur, in Bihar, heading towards central India. A dusty blur, mostly. One time, I started to piss on the road and realized that a woman grass-cutter was watching me from behind a bush. I had already let fly but the woman did not bat an eye, and went back to her work unperturbed. I thought that very sexy. The next time I relieved myself in the middle of nature, it was a guy on top of a bus who caught the full show. But he didn't seem impressed either.

Stopped to gas up. Then saw an attendant motioning me towards the diesel pump. I pointed to the petrol dispenser, but he insisted that I come to the diesel side. I took my bike there and he prepared to pour in diesel. Then the other pump attendants came to my rescue and gave me the proper fuel. Transpired that the fellow was sick in the head. Heaven knew what he was doing there. Maybe the owner had a sick sense of humour. Maybe he will still be laughing when the moron burns down his pump.

Kishanganj to Purnea is a banana belt. Huge piles of the fruit were kept on the road for transportation. I saw mostly children carrying and selling the bananas to passing motorists.

Strange sights, like those of men on bicycles carrying radios on shoulder straps, can still be seen in rural areas.

These images have long been wiped away from the memories of us city types. Buses and other public transport are overwhelmed by the sheer numbers of commuters. People hang out of these vehicles, perch on the bonnets of the jeeps, even the tops of buses. Three to four times the number of authorized passengers travel in these vehicles. The blaring music from these vehicles can be heard for miles around. The gaily decorated tractors are a sight to see. There seems to be continuous competition for the most garish contraption and also for the loudest music possible. Goats being ferried in gunny bags on cycles was a new one for me.

I passed this vision with long hair, white beard and some sort of robe, carrying a staff. Like some long-ago saint come to life. I passed by him slowly but he was in a world of his own. I had no business intruding. A seeker passed by in my life.

Bhagalpur is a big town and I halted on the outskirts for a four-hundred-buck stay. There was no parking but they had a system for chaining bikes in position, and had a night guard, which satisfied me. This had been another long day and Marco Polo's son deserved the rest.

I had my bike unchained and on the road by 5.30 in the morning. The small towns in this part of the country still have paved roads inside. So you bump your way in the town and come out to the tarred portion outside. Where the tar still adheres, that is.

Breakfast in a dhaba with a huge number of people hovering around the bike. A trucker gave me directions and confused me further. He was talking short cuts, and I was not interested, but one listens and learns. Meanwhile I ate thick, solid rotis with dal and potato-fry. I've noticed Biharis love to eat potato deep-fried. Tasty, no doubt, but it goes straight to the midriff of fat people like me. Most of the people were friendly. Contrary to popular belief, mindless violence does not happen all the time in Bihar. I was greeted and treated well in that state of earthy people. You just didn't act funny with them—or you lay yourself open to losing a limb or two.

A town called Akbarpur had blaring speakers, the kind that is barred in most places now, spewing forth bhajans. The entire town was soaked in music. The heat, dust and noise were jarring. Maybe the noise had something to do with intimidating a certain community.

The only time on the entire journey that I took a wrong turn, I landed in the town of Gaya instead of Bodhgaya. Gaya is an old town with serpentine alleyways and I was well and truly lost. The clogged streets did not give me enough time to ask for proper directions, nor to receive a proper answer. I was just carted along with the general flow of traffic, getting further enmeshed in the town. An old karmic friend took pity on me and personally went out of his way on his motorcycle to lead me out of the labyrinth I had trapped myself in. Whew! That was a pointless one-hour during which I felt well and truly helpless.

Back on course and the open roads were a relief. Stopped to ask for directions at an army checkpoint.

Reghu, the soldier, had to be from Kerala because he recognized the number-plates from his state. We volleyed questions and answers and swapped stories. The fellow was homesick and hearing his mother tongue was a treat for him. He was reluctant to let me go, but go, I had to. A sentimental soldier about to cry on your shoulder is not a pretty sight and the army brass is liable to frown on it.

A joker on a bike stopped to enquire about my health and I told him to fuck off, which he did. Gaya is supposed to be violence-prone and I had made sure to make it to Bodhgaya in time. Busloads of pilgrims from Sikkim have been looted in the night-time in this area. Fortunately, none have been killed so far but plenty have been burgled and beaten up. I'd met the victims of these unfortunate incidents back home, so I was extra careful.

I went straight to the Mahabodhi Society, which had booked me in a hotel way above my budget. But the parking looked good and I gave in to the temptation of a comfortable room. I was to have stayed at the Society's guest house but I had asked for the bookings too late. The Tibetans who ran the hotel I put up at had yet to open their restaurant and I had to go out to eat. Bodhgaya, where the Buddha gained enlightenment. A major destination had been reached today.

26

I seem to come to this place during major upheavals in my life. The last time was with my father's ashes. Bewildered and disoriented, I had limped into this holy place and gone back with a measure of self-confidence and gifts—I came to discover later—that would last me a lifetime. Crisis time and my footsteps lead to this place.

After a quick bath I headed for the sanctum sanctorum. Slipping quietly inside, I saw a Tibetan nun, a Sri Lankan monk and a Japanese lady quietly reciting their prayers. An hour or so passed in contemplation and meditation. I felt the disturbance in me magnified by the calmness of the shrine. I was dimly aware of people silently coming in and out. Hushed voices and reverence walk hand in hand.

There was a small commotion in the back and I turned to see an old monk prostrate himself at the shrine three times, with great difficulty, refusing help from anybody. I knew he was a Rimpoche or great teacher not just by his retinue but by the aura that surrounds such masters. The old man entered the main shrine and recited a prayer in a voice cracked with reciting hundreds and thousands of prayers and mantras for a lifetime. He went on for a long time and I felt that he was saying a goodbye and a thank-you. It was an experience, being in the main shrine with a Master praying his heart out. Kensur Rimpoche Jumpa Yeshe gave the Tibetan nun and me a blessing on his way out. I'd been at the right place at the right time for once.

Going around the shrine, I noticed several young men and women who just sat along the wall, looking into nothingness. I joined their ranks. Under the Bodhi tree, groups of laymen and women and monks and nuns from different parts of the world were praying. Sermons were also given by monks to their respective groups. Burmese, Sri Lankans, Thais, Japanese, Tibetans, Indians, Cambodians, Nepalese, Chinese, Americans and Europeans, all went about their business without fuss or desperation. There was no need to enforce order in such a crowd. They carried it inside them.

But there was this Thai monk, who seemed to be a regular at the temple, who got into an argument with an employee of the Society. The monk clearly had some marbles missing, shouting as he was under the Bodhi tree and on the verge of getting violent. I had to intervene and put an end to the unholy incident. The Society employee said that the monk was mad. I later saw him leading the prayers for his group in a hypnotic voice and with a serene expression on his face. The mad monk of Bodhgaya.

Then there was this beautiful young European woman who spent all her time on the premises in walking meditation. You could not help but notice her, what with that radiant loveliness. Sadly, I found her sitting outside chemists' shops all over Bodhgaya, always in a daze. A deeply distressed drug addict.

Monks, nuns and lay people alike waited under the Bodhi tree to collect leafs, twigs and seeds that fell at regular intervals. I collected a few leaves too.

Night time saw a raggedy band of protesters on the main street. A torchlight procession of hawkers who had been evicted from the streets.

The day I was to leave, I went to meditate among the stupas along the outer perimeter early in the morning. Lovely. Tibetan lamas sometimes stay here the whole night, doing their prostrations, or meditating under mosquito nets. I felt some of the silt in my mind settle to the bottom. I left Bodhgaya with the Master's prayer singing in my ears.

27

Next stop would have to be found on the way. I really had no idea where I would halt, only the general direction I would be taking. I planned to try and connect to the highway which cleanly bisects India. So, from Bihar, it would be through Jharkhand into Chhattisgarh. My road map was ragged in the extreme. I tried to work out the distances and gave up.

Away I went towards Aurangabad. The road was surprisingly good, until the dirt track started at Hariharganj which was on the Jharkhand border. Just a few odd vehicles here with no other road to take and idiots like me who don't find the time to think things over. The bollocking my poor ass got was not funny. Forget the body, even the mind grew numb. To top it all, puncture number three. Lucky me, I found a repairman just a kilometre away. The fellow was being berated by another customer in a van with a puncture. He was being accused of strategically placing nails on the road. We thought alike, the gentleman in the van and me. Not a gentleman actually, most probably the big dad of the area. With his curling moustache above a sneering red mouth fringed with paan, he was not a pretty sight. The mechanic went about his work quietly. Venom vented, Red Lips turned his attention to me. My size and rough appearance caused him to treat me with some respect. He probed and I lied. He probed some more and I lied some more. With his tyre repaired and a parting abuse at the poor man, he gave me a baleful look and went on with his life.

This was a desperately poor part of India. Shops were few and far between; I ran out of water and did not get to lay my hands on a bottle of mineral water for close to 150 kilometres. Dehydration was a distinct possibility that day. Lunch was a couple of samosas from a run-down cart. I sat on the bike and ate what was there in the open air. I was more interested in the tea. At least that was boiled water, hopefully free of stomach bummers. One young mother of five came and argued about the price of the samosas. Two rupees per piece upset her budget but one-fifty was fine. The owner relented and sold them at her price. I think he had been there before and the poor are understanding of their own kind.

On one of my stops in the countryside I was accosted by a very old man who asked me for some *khaini*, chewing tobacco popularly shared among the poorer classes. I offered him a cigarette, and he lit it as he would a beedi. Beedi-smokers usually first hold the tip to the flame, and once that gets going, they inhale. Imagine, an old man smoking his first cigarette about a step away from death. That's poverty for you. No wonder the Maoists are having a field day in this area. As a thank-you, the old man said giving a man a smoke was considered dharma in his village. I suspect he was not right in the head.

Near a place called Rampur, I had to stop for a herd of goats to cross the road. Since I had to stop, I decided to enjoy the break. The old and wizened goatherd wished me, 'Jai Ram, Sahib' and I wished him back in the same words. I would have paid a million dollars for the smile that elicited from him; a brilliant flash. It was a Zen moment for me. We'd only exchanged a couple of words and a smile, and yet, something moved somewhere.

Some dozen thugs were collecting donations at a forest checkpost, ostensibly to conduct a puja. They were in connivance with the staff of the forest department. It was all very official; I was ordered to switch off my engine and asked for my papers. I saw some sort of a receipt in the hands of the johnnie who was acting the most officious. I knew by then that this was a rip-off. Declaring myself to be an IAS officer (retirement was kept a secret), I tore into those pricks. The forest guards were threatened with suspension and I demanded to see the written permission for collecting donations. Pulling out my mobile I pretended to speak to a senior police officer and the district magistrate of the area. I'd spoilt their party and they literally begged me to depart. The magic of the service works with these thugs every time. Another blow on behalf of the proletariat.

Garwha, in Jharkhand, was an eye-opener. I had stopped to ask directions from a policeman. He advised me not to talk to anyone on the roads and not to take on a pillion under any circumstances. I saw plainclothesmen with self-loading rifles, and cartridge belts across their chests. This proclaimed them to be some sort of paramilitary force. I saw many of them on the road in town, and in vehicles. This area is part of the 'red corridor' where the Maoists are ruling the roost in the rural areas. Desperate times and desperate men.

I arrived in the town of Ambikapur in the evening and just faded into sleep. As always, I left early the next day. The target for the day was to reach Jabalpur, where I would finally catch the national highway in the central part of India. The Chhattisgarh side of the journey was fine, with good roads, and the Chota Nagpur plateau is beautiful to ride across. The early morning fog was a surprise and I even had to take out a jacket. During the course of the day I kept consulting the tattered map, making new configurations, eventually deciding to head instead for Mandla in Madhya Pradesh as it afforded a more southern direction and I could meet the highway at Seoni.

Breakfast on the road was a couple of vadas. The chutney looked like vomit and the vada tasted like mud. The vomit was tasty and I asked for a second helping.

Good old bike was acting up. Stuttering and stalling, it died on me just outside Baikunthapur. The roadside mechanics were still to open shop. While waiting I fiddled with the wiring, and lo and behold, it started working fine. I decided to push my luck and ride ahead.

I kept going till I reached Baikunthapur in search of a professional second opinion. This mechanic was the one who was lying in wait for me, the fraud I expected to meet sooner or later who would prove to be the antithesis of the hallowed beings I'd encountered earlier on the road. He did essentially the same things I'd done to the wiring a couple of hours ago. He pulled and he pushed. All the while he tried to distract me with small talk and useless advice on how to treat the bike. I was not convinced by his pronouncement of the fitness of the bike. He was a fellow with a fancy hairstyle and aspirations to be in the movies, I thought. But since the bike was still moving well, I held my tongue and left his shack.

There is a shanty or two at Kabir junction, in the middle of the forest on the border between Chhattisgarh and Madhya Pradesh. Lunch was some pakoras and a fist full of bhujiya. Today was not a day for culinary heights. There was this truck-driver eating the same lunch. He had a truck fully loaded with the trunks of sal trees. He informed me about the loading process. All done by hand, imagine that!

Then began a terrible road through the forest. It was a downhill ride on loose pebbles. Hell, for a biker. At times I literally had to walk the motorcycle. I could also feel an eerie presence around me. It was the middle of the day but I was quaking in my pants. This was definitely not a happy forest. I took refuge in my mantra and was hugely relieved when civilization reappeared.

I was lucky that the bike had held out in the jungle,

because it conked out again near the village of Chabi-kheri in the evening. The only mechanic there identified the problem, changed the fuse and all was well. With relief I went to a puja pandal to which some local boys who had befriended me while I was waiting for the bike to be repaired, had invited me. They shouted 'Jai Mata Di' as I arrived, and I shouted the same back to them and the shouting went back and forth for some time. I can understand how hard-core fundamentalists freak out. This sort of shouting leads you into a frenzy. The group of friendly young villagers crowded around me, eager to make small talk with the fanatical stranger they took me to be. Religion bound us together and for the moment I became the 'traveller to temples'. From the Vaishno Devi shrine to the temples of Madurai, I spun stories for those hungry ears. I have actually had occasion to visit these holy places, so it wasn't all made up. With a tilak the size of a cricket bat on my forehead, and another shouting frenzy, I was on my way.

Mandla is a town which leaves no imprint on the mind. I had reached it at seven in the evening and the only thing I remember about it is the dirty goop in the sink of the forlorn hotel I stayed in. They have an odd practice at small hotels. You are presented with soaps, small to begin with, but further cut in half for use. Even the paper napkins, if any, are cut into small strips.

28

It was one hell of a ride from Mandla to Adilabad, through a portion of Madhya Pradesh and a part of Maharashtra, right to the tip of Andhra Pradesh. Breakfast was at a roadside eatery proudly advertising 'The Centre for Sexual Studies; Maharajpur; District Mandla'. There was the vendor, his wife and a goat. The woman was eyeing me surreptitiously the whole time. It looked like she had taken the course advertised proudly in her shop and was keen to practise what it preached. The goat chewed at the lime on the pillars. The man cooked my rotis and eggs, keeping an eye all the while on his wife.

The area around Nagpur was festooned with Buddhist flags and someone was giving a fiery speech somewhere. Must have been a convention of neo-Buddhists. Even vehicles bore flags. It was almost a political scene. I guess practices differ in different places.

There was a lot of drinking going on, on the road.

People would stop on the roadside and drink straight from the bottle. Not beer, mind you, but whisky and rum. I had some oily food in a shady bar and treated myself to a bottle of beer in compensation for the heat of the day. Some men came and parked their vehicle, asked for water and glasses, sat in their vehicles, drank rapidly and zoomed away. All this *outside* a bar. What's with these characters and boozing in vehicles?

The person who was serving me was practically a dwarf. He barely came above the table but was adept at his job. Serving me and others with his hands above his head. Banging the glasses and bottles down on the table, he strode away for his next delivery. I was a bit disconcerted in the beginning to be served by this man, but later on I enjoyed the novelty of the situation. It's not every day you get served by the little people. I left him a huge tip by my standards. He smiled and winked at me.

I was on the main highway now, and actually speeding, in comparison to my previous few weeks' riding. Cutting across the middle of India towards the south again was thrilling. I planned to surprise a lot of people in Kerala.

On the way there was a sea of cows blocking the road. A full five minutes' halt. There must have been at least twenty men prodding the cattle onward. I had never seen anything like this before. Awesome sight. I worried about a stampede and looked for a place to hide in case of one. The only thing to do would be to climb onto the truck behind me. Plans in place, I waited for the onrush of hooves. Paranoid as usual. Nothing happened and we all went our respective ways.

The highways are murder for stray dogs. I'd seen the poor animals splattered on the concrete everywhere. Crows enjoy the pickings and the rest is slowly ground to dust by the vehicles. Among the slain on my trip were a cat and two deer. And a human body. Smashed cars and trucks were a common sight. The rescue and recovery scene is still in a very primitive stage. If you have a serious accident, the chances are that you will die before they get you to a hospital.

The traffic cop at Adilabad pointed me to a hotel. He was a friendly, jovial sort who asked me a lot of questions and looked genuinely interested in my journey. Intermittently, he insisted on shaking my hand. The last handshake lasted a long time. He was one of those classic hand-grabbers who can't let go. I wondered if he was gay.

The hotel was an indescribable hole, with a toilet. The ashtray had not been cleaned in a decade. The curtains belonged to the Nehru era and the carpet had fused with the concrete floor. The bedsheets were almost transparent with washing, but clean. The towel was just a rag. The mirror was dirty and cracked and the electric sockets were falling out of the walls. The fan moved with a creaking sound and was liable to fall off the ceiling any time. The door had to be banged shut and the bolt was so rusted, it was screaming blood-poisoning. The bathroom had a shower which didn't work. The water came in a trickle. Asking for hot water would seem like telling a joke. The shit pot was, shall we say, full of shit. The basin contained material I did not care to identify. And the bathroom floor bore the hair of yesterday's users. There, I'm done with describing the indescribable.

It wasn't a lot different in hotel after hotel round the country. Travelling, my friend, especially on a small budget, is a filthy business.

I had a serious problem on my hands. Literally. The knuckles on both the hands had swollen and were positively arthritic in the mornings. I had to do some slow warming-up exercises before I could open and close my fist. The constant ten-to-twelve-hour rides had begun to take their toll. The old body was cracking up and I just hoped it would hold for a month more, by which time I would have wound up this crazy part of my life. I thought the back would go first but it was the fingers that let me down. The fingers of an artist that had been fashioned by nature to do nothing more than fondle a woman's breasts— and sometimes ply a quill—could not take the everyday brutality of the harsh handles of a motorcycle.

Another thumb rule of the road. The smaller and cheaper the hotel, the more suspicious the management is of you. I've learnt to offer an advance even before being asked for it.

The old receptionist at the Adilabad hotel was obviously also the owner and I got talking to him in Hindi. I asked him the reason for the lack of trust in customers. 'Asking for an advance is a bit rude, don't you think?' I wondered aloud. Shrewd businessman that he was, he began by saying that my 'kind of people' did not frequent his hotel. Almost fifty per cent of those who came there didn't have the money to pay up. Which was why half the customers walked away when the advance was demanded. This was news to me.

He went on and on about the travails of his business, about people not paying for the food, about people stealing things, about people destroying property and defecating in the room, and other such horror stories. Seems I had a touched a raw nerve and the woes of a lifetime gushed out. He was so caught up by my sympathetic ear, he even followed me to my room, bleating all the way—until I shut the door in his face.

Adilabad to Kurnool was 520 kilometres and took twelve hours—with an unintended hour in Hyderabad, owing to being given the wrong directions by a person of illegitimate birth. I was heading towards the Mumbai road. Over the months, I had learnt to read the movements of the sun, and the direction in which I was headed was usually pretty clear to me. I'd figured something was not quite right and, after double-checking with the great god in the sky, I veered back.

Trying to eat on the road, with monkeys snatching at things, can pose quite a challenge. A big dhaba I'd come to was fair witness to a running battle between humans and simians. It employed a chap for the sole purpose of chasing away our small cousins. I wondered how he felt, chasing monkeys for a living. A big 'un grabbed a packet of chips from someone, tore it open, crunched up the contents, and scratched his balls with satisfaction. Impressive performance, that. The previous proprietor of the chips shook with impotent rage and cuffed the monkey-chaser for dereliction of duty.

Nearly every vehicle I saw in Andhra Pradesh was festooned with garlands, flowers and assorted greenery. It looked like the forest had taken to the road. Entire shrubberies, zipping by. I concluded it was festival time. I was busy fobbing off hitchhikers. Some of them were pretty aggressive, leaping onto the road right in front of me, demanding a ride. The fuckers believed in their right to a ride. Just can't understand this country.

Saw a lot of beggars on the road today. Or maybe I noticed them for the first time. Men, women and children. Broken arms, broken legs and broken spirits. Begging children really depress me. They deserve better so early in their lives. One chap I met to ask for directions asked me for some money. He looked well fed and pretty well dressed. I don't know why, but I gave him a hundred bucks. Thamzi.

Mad people were also there in plenty. These wild, unwashed and vacant-eyed people fascinate me. What do they think about? How do their minds work? Is their reality more real than ours? Are they really the lucky ones? Are they cosmically more connected? I confess I am respectful of these people and acknowledge their presence with deference. Passing them on the road, I feel the need to bow slightly. You never know who is an evolved soul. Can't take chances with the Buddha. Bet you think I'm qualified to join their elite club. Maybe.

I tried out a hotel in a place called Madhepura, in Andhra Pradesh. Even by my now extremely low standards, the room I was given was the pits. The sheets bore ample evidence of their last use. I could hear the semen shouting with joy in expectation of fresh company.

The late lunch in this town was no joy either. The biryani was greasy and altogether horrible. The only saving grace was the boiled egg that topped it. Even the cook could not interfere with that.

Some places have it and some don't. Madhepura didn't.

Since the traffic was heavy and it was night, I had difficulty with the bright headlights continuously beamed right in my eyes. I found that riding between two trucks was the best bet because I could thereby escape the glare from the traffic coming towards me. I would put this discovery to use many times in the future.

Finally reached Kurnool and bedded down. The hotel kitchen was shut down, in deference to the festive mood, and the waiter had to get the food from outside—which was fine by me. Only problem was that when he came back with the food, two other waiters also sauntered casually into the room. As if this was the waiter's common room. I imagined them at any moment sitting down to make themselves at home, and kidding back and forth with me. 'Fuck off!' I yelled. It was in English, but they appeared to get the gist. Also, I didn't have to tip the waiter.

I was so cheesed off, I dug out my Swiss knife the next morning and got to work on the underside of the mattress. They would remember me sometime later.

29

Bangalore was a city I should have got to months ago. But, hey, a free mind is allowed to roam without reason, without the should-haves and the must-haves. Kurnool— of the savaged mattress fame—was left behind in a cloud of dust, and a nasty exchange of glances, early in the morning. The invasion of my privacy still rankled. I should have shown them my real privates.

The food I'd had in Kurnool proved—belatedly—so good that I had the runs and I employed the now familiar roadside to empty myself, looking around carefully all the while for snakes.

There was this Sardar with a huge empty dhaba in the middle of nowhere. It was between breakfast and lunchtime, so I opted for brunch. The cook killed everything, including the eggs. The mystery of the empty dhaba was cleared.

I.S.N. Prasad is a dear friend and, unfortunately, is still

working for the government. His wife Vandita is also a dear friend and she shares that misfortune in her choice of profession. '*I want to break free*' was their signature tune a decade ago. Now they will run the gamut of middle age and retirement. They may just break free.

I invited myself to their beautiful house, after having submitted the motorcycle for a major look-at to a garage-owner who was reluctant to take on the job because of the time frame I'd requested. The house seemed unprepossessing from the outside but was wonderfully airy and well designed inside. Vandita can watch goings-on in the entire house from her vantage point, her computer station on the first floor. No wonder Prasad's shoulders stoop some more and he is also balding under that constant gaze. Their children study at an alternate school which has only sixty-five students and eighteen teachers. The Prasads are that kind of people.

My huge pile of dirty clothes was slipped to the horrified maid, who was clearly unused to such quantities of soil in this house. But she was an employee of not one, but two bureaucrats, and had learnt her lessons well. She quickly recovered, slipped on the mask of an obedient servant, and did an efficient job, just like her employers.

We jawed about life, the service, religion, gossip surrounding batchmates, and the state of the nation. It was such a diversion talking to well-read people with myriad interests. The great food and the single-malt constituted a mere bonus. What a pleasure to have a bath in hot water and to have a clean bed to sleep in. Certain pleasures of life had become magnified. I'd never again take them for granted. I slept away an entire day. *Really* slept.

The next evening I went to pick up the motorcycle. I was held up at the garage for a few hours as the work had not finished. This was the authorized workshop of the manufacturing company, and I saw row upon row of gleaming bikes in waiting. I wandered around, looking at the countless extra fittings to be had. Today, we have it all. Every comfort to go with a two-wheeler, except, maybe, an attached bed.

Some boys were waiting for their machines and we got talking. Age does not matter when there is a common interest. They were impressed with what I was doing and I laid my exploits on thick. Adulation makes me heady. The boasting ended with the presentation of the bill. The chain had been changed, the back light strap had been replaced, new indicators too had been put in, the usual servicing done on the cut-out and fuses, and more. Big bill, which I met—and headed out into a drizzle. Of course, it was only the drenching and the Bangalore traffic that made me attack Prasad's single malt with renewed relish. Blame anybody, and anything, for a drink.

The Prasads are interested in religion, and Vandita, in particular, is into meditation. She had heard about Vipassana meditation and I explained it as best as I could. My knowledge was very limited and this was dangerous ground to tread. I thought the Prasad home was a good place in which to leave one of the leaves I'd collected from the Bodhi tree, and the present was accepted with the right amount of awareness. Great couple. Great friends.

I realized that I had neglected to renew my acquaintance with the famous spots of this city of pubs. I had been to Bangalore umpteen times before and hit the pubs with single-minded doggedness. Bangalore without a pubbing spree! Unthinkable, till last year! Some things change and I had crossed a certain line sometime since.

30

I headed further south to my foster home, Kerala. The
regular way would have been through Madurai to
Thiruvananthapuram. That morning's drizzle was a mood-
dampener and I abruptly opted for an entry into Kerala the
same day. I was homesick, I realized with some
astonishment. So I drove towards Mandya in Karnataka
and Wynad in Kerala. The bloody road just stopped.
There was absolutely nothing ahead. *Déjà vu. Orissa.* I was
on the highway to Madurai around five in the morning.
The spanking new highway had huge signs declaring the
destinations and on an impulse, I took the one towards
Mandya. There was no traffic on this road and I began to
get a little worried. I lit a pensive cigarette. Stood around
in the drizzle cursing myself for my impulses. By and by
a one-ton vehicle approached and I asked for directions.
The smiling driver asked me to follow him on a dirt track
for a couple of kilometres and I was finally on the highway
to Kerala.

Mysore is a beautiful city but I had been there many times and so took a diversion outside it. The roads in south India are far better than those in most of the rest of the country. All other common indices of development are also much better: lower infant mortality, lower fertility rates, improved health in general, improved education, communications and housing.

Bangalore, on the contrary, had proved disappointing. The city had grown like an uncontrolled giant in the past decade but did not have the infrastructure to deal with the boom in information technology. Clogged roads and a general shabbiness gave away the inside story.

I was inside the Kerala border by noon. That part of the road was through forestland and was quiet and serene, with less traffic than I'd grown used to. I was fortunate to see some deer grazing. I used to travel this road frequently when importing milk for north Kerala almost fifteen years ago. Those days there was a serious shortage of milk in the area and my job was to somehow make up the difference to an increasingly marauding public. Many of the vendors had been beaten up, due to the short supply. Mandya, in Karnataka, had milk to spare and so I had to go to beg for milk from time to time. The Karnataka Milk Federation had its own shortages in other places, but I was given milk to tide over the crisis in north Kerala only because the boss of the milk federation was from Mizoram, on the same side of the country as my home state, and of Mongol stock for good measure. That is why he took pity on the whining young officer before him. This story has been lying buried deep inside my heart for a long time, and now that it's out in the public domain, I hope I am not hounded by the Official Secrets Act.

Both my eye-drop containers have holes in them. I don't know how they got that way. Rats, maybe. I will just have to suffer till I reach a decent-size town. Gritty eyes are very uncomfortable.

I stopped at a KFC outlet. Kedda Fried Chicken. And they sold 'broasted' chicken too. Top that, American KFC. What the hell was broasted chicken? Boiled chicken, I supposed, that had subsequently been roasted. There was a busload of giggling college girls eating lunch under the watchful eye of two stern-faced nuns. I wonder why nuns have to look so serious. Loving Jesus should make them smile. I didn't like the suspicious looks the present two were giving me, either. Did they think I was about to molest their charges?

I ordered the standard Kerala 'meal'. In this part of the country it is never lunch, always a meal. Rice, rasam, veggies, buttermilk, sambar, pappadam and fish usually go to make it up. I had no desire to suffer the beady eyes of the nuns nor the curious looks of the tittering group, so I sat at a table outside facing away from them. The view was suddenly blocked by a macho bus driver. Without formality or invitation, he plonked himself on the other side of my table and proceeded to show off his broken Hindi. I took an immediate dislike to the boor and shocked him by unleashing what was, in comparison, my excellent Malayalam. That unsettled him and he blinked rapidly. Then I began to—in my newly cultivated habit—lie to him with abandon. I was an officer of the Central Bureau of Investigation on a mission and it was better he did not ask too many questions. Wink, wink. He blinked some more. Told him in a hoarse whisper that funny things were afoot. Wink-wink. I grilled him about his job, his employer, what they charged for hiring out the bus; everything I could think of. With a final cautionary word to keep his eyes open, I left the man fingering his thick moustache like one in a dream. I then went on to eyeball the nuns with a lecherous look, to their horror, and to the amusement of the bolder gigglers. Lunch was, after all, an enjoyable experience.

I stopped in the town of Kalpetta to buy my eye-drops and a crowd gathered, as usual. I have noticed all over India that there are a standard number of roles played by the members of a crowd. There are a couple of curious questioners, a few who can't keep their hands off the machine, one or two wise guys who have all the answers, fans of the wise guys, general nodders and plain gawpers.

Where are you from? Sikkim, I declared. Yeah, it's near Thailand, said the day's wise guy. How did you know? I asked. Smirk, smirk. The wise guys also inevitably know all about motorcycles. Even this new model. They would have taken mine for a spin and been impressed by its performance. I have seen this skit all over the country and it is the same, give or take local colour.

Further up, I stopped to buy a bottle of mineral water and the garrulous shopkeeper kept plying me with questions.

The people of this state are naturally curious and the fact that I speak the lingo makes me a natural target of questions. No one approached me in my previous avatar, because I was this conservatively dressed individual emerging from a government vehicle. Now, with my long hair, baggy clothes, motorcycle and biking gear, I presented a curious spectacle, and everyone felt free to learn more about me. This time I decided to be a scientist from the VSSC space control station in Thiruvananthapuram. There seemed to have been a raging controversy reported in the newspapers over a section of land in that area. The mineral water man eagerly asked me for the inside story. If I had known something about it I would have spun a yarn. Having no idea, I pretended to be an absent-minded scientist not involved in earthly matters, and scooted from there before anyone penetrated my disguise.

My fingers were troubling me in the daytime too. The pain was severe enough to affect my driving. Every time I pressed the clutch, I felt shooting pains in the left hand, and the right hand cramped up frequently. I could only ignore this at my own peril. I'd have to think about ending the trip. Sad, but I had to listen to my own body.

A small hotel with a grand name was my resting ground for the night. (I had made it a policy not to put up at, as far as possible, any government guest houses throughout my journey. I wanted a clear distance from government establishments of any sort.) I turned on the television and back were the same faces spouting the same messages. Politics dominates the airwaves and the same liars were sitting around smugly, looking deeply serious about many issues on the burner. I even heard mention of the Supreme Court case in which I'd been charged with contempt of court. Welcome back to Kerala.

31

Familiar territory. I'd come back to Thiruvananthapuram after a gap of some months, having traversed the country twice from the south to the north and twice from the east to the west. With swollen fingers to show for it. And a depleted wallet. But I was happy to meet Kuttapan, of mother-in-law fame. He had prepared a sumptuous lunch replete with all the food I would die for. Karimeen, a local fish, was the queen of the feast. There was also, among several other dishes, seer fish, fish curry and tapioca. I dined on for an hour and a half. Sheela, wife of Kuttapan and a senior official in my old service, made a quick lunchtime entrance and getaway. Back to her onerous duties as Secretary to the chief minister.

Over some beer, Kuttapan, Jony (Sheela's visiting elder brother who had settled in Chennai) and I talked of this and that. Kuttapan does not drink. The last time he had beer he lost his underpants in the swimming pool in the middle of the night. Today, he was not his normal self as there was an in-law in the house. I, on my part, grew maudlin drunk, relieved to have reached Thiruvananthapuram without my fingers falling off by the wayside.

The house, in which I'd been treated like family for many years, offered a major level of comfort. I could walk in any time and grab things from the fridge. Even the old lady who came to cook knew what my likes and dislikes were and she put special effort into the meals. We bonded well, and a few hundreds exchanged hands once in a while. Keep the cook happy, is my motto. Especially in houses where one is a self-invited guest frequently.

Kuttapan is a planter by profession. He visits his ancestral home infrequently, where his ninety-plus mother still rules the roost. He is the youngest of some twenty-two siblings from the same father but two different mothers. His mother has a football team of his siblings. With the result that there are over a hundred first cousins. The editor of the family newsletter has to be Kuttapan. The cousins are spread all over the world and the absurd newsletter is eagerly awaited, claims the editor. The claim has not been verified. One day, I tentatively suggested the appropriateness of a website and was summarily put in my place. Kuttapan still believes in the pleasure of touching and reading from paper. And maybe he's just not technology-friendly. As I recall, I have never seen him near a computer.

A man who counts eighty-year-olds among his cousins has to be somewhat conservative. Even though he is a mere kid of fifty-six at the time of writing, he has been breaking bread with the eighty- and seventy-year-olds—and sharing dirty jokes with them—for half a century. This demands respect and I surrender to age and experience. He will decide who his two sons will marry, right down to the brides' denomination. Twenty-five years ago, he pursued Sheela, who came from a different denomination altogether, but that was an aberration and the rules won't be broken again.

The elder boy, Renju, had been sent by Sheela to Sikkim for what she euphemistically called 'life training'. I assumed that I was to give the boy a hard time. So I made him work at all levels of the hotel hierarchy. One day, while doing the job of a driver, he drove my Gypsy off the road. For company he had a cook and four industrial gas cylinders. The lucky guy was rescued from a vehicle hanging on a stump of wood twenty feet below the road. Got away without a scratch. Death training, more likely. Now, he is having the time of his life in Ireland.

Kuttapan is the sort of character who wanted idlis in Gangtok. He would reject the local food with disdain and demand dosas, another impossible find in Sikkim. The rest of the family was adventurous and accommodating. But not our man. He was doing his best to get back at me for all the years of ragging. I understood and accepted. He could not wear his mundu in Sikkim or else his balls would have frozen. But he took care to project everything Malayalee about himself. On his fanatical days, he pronounced even Thiruvananthapuram to be a barely tolerable place to live in. The best of all possible worlds, he said, lay in Kanjirapally, his birthplace.

His system for keeping his in-laws at bay has been perfected stealthily over time. 'Operation at Bay' started from the first day of marriage. He has never admitted to it officially but over the years I have managed to glean this much of the story. Personality counted in his strategy. Show a deep reserve crammed with formality. Never exchange more than two formal sentences at a time. Give a break of at least four hours before the next exchange of formalities. Disappear for hours from the house, even if it means sitting alone in the movie halls like a pervert. Act very busy. Avoid eating meals together. Take off to another town for a few days. Serve the poisonous putte everyday. But maintain cordial relations. Never give them a chance to complain. And be very alert to when they are proposing to leave. Kuttapan always escorts his mother-in-law back to her house. He even stays overnight to ensure she stays put. I won't go into finer detail as it would put a strain on my friend's marriage.

This then was the gentleman I was lunching with. The man who once impressed me with a duck-eating performance at his uncle's house in the Kuttanad region of Kerala. This area is the rice bowl of Kerala and is below sea level. Ducks are abundant here, despite Kuttapan's raids on their population. Kuttapan had torn into two whole ducks using both hands with a silent savagery I hadn't associated with the man. The only noise was the cracking of bones and the chomping of flesh and the occasional grunt of satisfaction. Primal!

Sheela plays mother hen to the younger officers. I treat her as I would an elder sister and she treats me like the rogue I am. A calm temperament has seen her through life with Kuttapan. She is a well-regarded officer, a good wife and mother. An epitome of the modern Indian woman. She is one woman I have seen eating dinner standing up and straight from the fridge. That was a weird sight.

Friends dropped by the whole day. Abraham from next door had kept the sanctity of his name. Ideal son, ideal husband, ideal father and an excellent, if over-qualified bureaucrat. Engineer, with a management degree, and a financial analyst to boot, a graduate of the best Indian and foreign universities, he is lost in the politics of the day. Deeply religious, he attends church every morning after a five-kilometre run. Amachi, his mother, stitched my torn pants. This was instigated by Kuttapan and was an embarrassment for me. Abraham recommended an ayurvedic doctor for my swollen fingers.

Kuttapan was the first to bring up the topic of his ailments when he accompanied me to the doctor. I thought I was the patient but I realized I had a very sick person beside me. The doctor was a religious yeller. After a couple of sentences, he'd yell '*Daivamay!*' which literally translates as 'Oh, God!' I was dumbstruck by the fellow's antics, having been rendered speechless in the first place by Kuttapan's litany of woes. Then started the cautious progress to their respective family histories. Probing each other till they found a common branch on the tree, celebrated by another yell. I finally got my shot with the doctor and he plied me with medicines to swallow and oils to apply, accompanied by food and drink restrictions. He shooed us to the door with a final yell.

I wanted to have an ayurvedic masseur come in for the few days I was staying there. The man came to the house but the sicker person got first service and I had to wait for my turn. With the oil and the warm powder massage, it was not long before I felt the difference. Even my complexion cleared.

Kuttapan has the pulse of the housing society in his hands. His house is situated at a crossroads from where the entire colony can be seen. Any car or individual entering it is scanned immediately, and the person knows it. Kuttapan's station behind the window curtains is a colony secret.

32

Kovalam has been my favourite beach for ever. It is a mandatory stop on most of my travels, and I hit the same spots over and over again. Most of my grub is from the German Bakery.

This time the stay at Kovalam was only for a night and I had cabbed it all the way there, my bike needing the further ministrations of a mechanic. Indian roads are tricky and the Enfield is essentially an old technology in need of constant maintenance.

Kovalam beach has been for me a spot to wind down after some hard work. I have taken refuge in this lovely beach time and again. Kuttapan thinks that I used to come here to visit the whores. To each his own, I say. His suspicions had been aroused because I usually came here alone, and did not stay at the government guest house, which is perched on top of a hill and far away from the action. So Kuttapan suspected, and will suspect to his dying day that I was up to no good on the beaches of Kovalam.

This was also the beach where Vishwas Mehta's modesty was last seen walking into the sea two decades ago. He is a friend in the service and we all call him 'Handsome'. Not because we think he is, but at his insistence. The fellow genuinely believes he is God's gift to women in 'God's own country', a slogan of the government of Kerala. His cultured wife, Preeti, has become a good friend. I take the words out of her mouth and she has been putting wholesome vegetarian fare in mine. I have also taken delight in putting pressure on Vishwas's cocktail cabinet time and again. His sad survey of his dwindling stock used to give me a certainly bigger kick than the cheap booze he kept at home. The couple have been friends of mine for a lifetime.

Kurien is a strongly built ox of a man with a twisted finger, the result of botched-up surgical carpentry after an accident with a coconut macheté. Loud, brash and bordering on the crude, he is a warm, generous host. He organized a gathering of the batchmates in my honour. Handsome was there, of course. Father James came and latched himself to my fingers. He is a deeply pious man who guided us through the initial period of disorientation in the state. I have never heard a bad word issue from his mouth, and so, I took malevolent delight in talking dirty in his presence. My efforts usually fetched me a cuff from Father James.

My other batchmates, Chauhan, Reddy and Ravikanth

were out of the state. I remember Chauhan inaugurating a coconut tree-climbing school by shinning up a palm himself, and getting his face plastered all over the media for his pains. Reddy has made it in life. He does not want anything more than to climb the bureaucratic ladder at the appropriate times. These then were the people I jumped into service with in Kerala. We got married, children were born and raised, we got promoted together and watched each other's backs in the hurly-burly of administration.

Other good friends, such as Marapandian, Rishiraj Singh and Paul Antony have been my frequent hosts for years in Thiruvananthapuram. Isaac, my old chauffeur, fed me at his home. Everybody takes pity on a man without his family.

My bike had been taken for another round of tinkering before the last leg of the journey. I had been applying the ayurvedic oil on my fingers, and a week's rest had done a spot of good. The intake of the medicines from the yeller would start when I resumed my journey. There were too many food and drink restrictions to go with them.

33

Kuttapan insisted that I visit his ancestral house on the way out from Kerala, because God knew when I would be coming by next. My princely pension of ten thousand rupees was being deposited in the sub-treasury. With this comforting knowledge in my armoury, and Kuttapan clinging to my back, we headed for Kanjirapally, the centre of his world. Within half an hour Kuttapan's ass caught fire and the ride was frequently interrupted to douse the blaze in his buttocks.

There are different routes to Kanjirapally and Kuttapan chose the one through Adoor sub-division, which had been my first posting as a full-fledged officer. This was where I'd got my first taste of power, backed by a red light on my car. I used to surreptitiously peep out of the car window at night to check out the blinking dome. People had to know that the boss was on the move.

This had been the hunting-grounds of Retnamma, a

failed politician with evidently a lot of time on her hands, who specialized in harassing young officers from north India. She was a mentally unstable woman who used to fall in love with these men and had even adopted the surname of my predecessor. I was aware of her antics. She used to write long love letters to us, and a file had been opened to keep them in. Even love letters from a maniac are religiously filed by the system. I had gone through the letters haltingly, with an interpreter, as the love was declared in terrible handwriting in Malayalam. My knowledge of the language was practically nil then. She was poetic, I'll tell you that. She was also mildly pornographic and was ready for action. In one of her demented love letters she had declared herself ready to teach me Malayalam at my home and anything else that was required to be taught to young men. She would come to my house and I would have to chase her out of the compound with a stick. Her predations continued in the office and after two months of this nonsense I had her evicted physically from the premises. She wrote letters against me to the President of India, the Prime Minister and nearly everybody else down the line. They all came back to me for further action, which meant further filing. Retnamma and her unrequited lust.

Then there was this old man who would write any old nonsense on pieces of cigarette packets, throw them at my desk from a safe distance, and run away. This happened every day. Nobody knew what he was doing there.

Then, I remember the day a thief rushed through my

office, a crowd of men in hot pursuit. In through one door and out through the other. Me, with my mouth open all the while.

I remember, too, an under-trial demanding to be let out of jail and banging his head on the metal rods of the courtroom. Blood was gushing out of his forehead, and four or five policemen tried to stop him from killing himself. Me, with my mouth open all the while.

There was a rush of memories as I passed through Adoor. Things I had not thought about in decades.

Next stop was Pathnamthitta, the district headquarters. Another rush of memories. I started the first day of my career playing cards with the district collector and his cronies, and drinking whisky with him in the daytime. It was a Sunday and I had yet to sign up officially. The man called me over to his house and invited me to gamble and to drink. A dilemma in the first minute of reaching the town. This man was a difficult boss with a penchant for a hipflask. He played havoc with my idealism and my missionary zeal.

Then came Alok Sheel, a total opposite to the previous man. Cultured, soft-spoken and with a spine of steel, he restored much of my faith that had taken such an early beating.

Despite all the deathbed groans, Kuttapan did not die and we reached the centre of the world without a hitch. Kanjirapally is a nice plantation town. My friend's ninety-four-year-old mother was waiting for us and, after my customary greeting and gift of a silk scarf, we settled down to a meal fit for a king. She honoured me by serving me with her own frail hands. The dining table was a single rosewood piece, and could seat sixteen. Legend has it that only four such pieces were made in Kerala. Then I met Kuttapan's playful young cousins, all in their sixties and seventies. Tonychan and Babu were qualified planters and very cultured people. It was a shock to meet management graduates from top Indian colleges of the middle of the last century. Lovely people.

The food was plentiful and mostly meat of all varieties. The daytime stuffing ruled out dinner. For a change we talked soberly of life, death and children. A nice ending to a day full of closures.

The ride from Kanjirapally to Kasargod was my quickest ride on the motorcycle in Kerala. The roads were empty because there had been a bandh called for whatever reason. I even sneaked a piss on the national highway. There was no food on sale, but hey, you gain some and you lose some. Kuttapan's mother had insisted on giving me some cashew nuts and banana chips, which did just fine to stifle any hunger pangs.

One group of creeps was trying to stop traffic in Mallapuram district and I rode through the bastards. The second group stopped traffic in the district of Kasargod but it was evening and we were soon let through.

Today, on the west coast road, was a day without public transport and I was happy to give lifts to people who asked. Unlike some other states, Kerala provides a safe community and there was no hesitation on my part. The only problem was the constant barrage of questions from the back which had to be dodged adroitly. I started lying as usual, with wild stories I'm too embarrassed to repeat.

I passed the house where I had stayed for a year in Kozhikode. A memory here and there filtered through my mind. I passed the office and the house where I had worked and stayed in Kannur as the district collector. I had to detour to do this but since I was making good time and the roads were empty, I decided to go for it. It was probably the last time I'd see these places, anyway. Two young men asked me for some petrol on the road. I gave them some from my motorcycle. I was in a generous mood.

Kasargod was the town of my training. Not much of a town, even today. I went to the hotel where I'd done little else than eat peas-fry and listen to sad music for months. It was closed down, not surprisingly. Change was all around and I found out that all the offices had relocated. As a matter of form I drove around the buildings that held the offices in the old days, and the few roads that I knew.

Dusk was settling in and I found a swanky new hotel in Kasargod, in which I spent my last night in Kerala. That night I did a lot of thinking. I had entered Kerala through Mangalore and I was exiting it through the same place. I wondered about the twenty years that had gone by in a flash, and thanked all the gods that be in Kerala for seeing me through them.

34

Hugging the western coast of Karnataka, I travelled on a dug-up highway. Expansion near Mangalore had played hell into the roads. I saw a breed of cows smaller than my motorcycle, real midgets, and I wondered how much milk they gave.

This was the famous Udupi heartland. The cuisine of this place has captured the hearts of millions of Indians, and restaurants claiming to be Udupi can be found anywhere in the country. I ate an excellent vegetarian lunch. These people really know how to cook. The combination of rice, sambar, vegetables, curd and pickles is finger-licking good. Throw in good service and a clean environment and you have a winner on your hands.

While I was waiting for the food I made my usual perambulations around the bike. For some reason, as I squatted near the bike, my attention was time and again drawn towards the saddlebags. I found the angle of the bags all wrong. I tried to rectify the angle when I found a big tear on one of the bags. Fortunately, none of the gear had fallen out and I only had to use some netting to hold the bag together for the day. This is the sort of sixth sense one develops on the road.

A twelve-hour ride to Canacona, in Goa. Goa is very different to the rest of India. The religion, dress, the emancipation of its women, its architecture and its ocean of bars, all set it apart. The roads are narrower but well kept. A drunk pointed me towards a hotel near the beach. The waiter was a hummer and a bumbler but he understood the orders. Extracting information from this chap was a no-no, however. All my efforts to know more about Canacona were rebuffed pleasantly with a hum and a mumble. The result was, I ended up eating some food in that cheap hotel that I'd like to forget.

Having a bath at the end of a long ride had become the highlight of each day. Seeing dark water trickle down my body was a pleasure. The dirt and the grime had become daily adversaries, but every day, I ended up winning the battle. The bath was usually with a bucket and mug, as my kind of budget didn't allow for a shower, unless it was broken. The odd working shower I'd encountered, I'd used sparingly, as I'm into conservation.

I have begun to realize over the years that I need less

and less of everything. I have stopped using aftershave and perfumes. I have very few clothes and tend to go on wearing them till they fall apart or are stolen. Yes! My clothes are still worth stealing.

I eat less. The wastage of water and electricity are my chief reasons for shouting at everyone at home. Kids today are so careless about consumption. Computers, music sets and other electronic items are just left on without being used, and that gets me into a frenzy. Over time, I've become an environmental-friendly being.

Patnim beach in this small town is just starting to grow. The tourist season was around the corner and preparations were on in full swing. The beach looked robust and large. I did not try the water as it was too early in the morning. I had my beard hacked off by a barber from Azamgarh, in Uttar Pradesh, who almost cried with relief at having found someone to speak Hindi to. I am unlucky with barbers and seem to pick the ones with the least steady hands and the foulest breath.

I had spotted a white man eying me back at Kovalam beach, but I'd dismissed him from my thoughts as just another homosexual who wasn't about to get lucky with me. As luck would have it, there he was again, as if he'd tailed me to Goa, looking at me suggestively while I hurriedly swallowed my breakfast. There were barely ten tourists in Patnim beach and he had to be one of them. I marched away in a pointed huff.

The ride to Panaji, the capital, was easy and smooth. Coconut palms all the way.

Frank is a dark-skinned Goan with a fat and ugly wife, and surprisingly sexy daughters. Flirting outrageously was a way of life with them. Frank and his wife looked on indulgently while the girls played havoc with my mind. This may have been mere business strategy, to keep the guests aroused and around. But I began to detect possibilities of an entanglement, especially with the elder daughter who told me she was twenty-three and looked more than available. Frank runs a small cottage-type hostelry just by the Baga beach. I was more than willing to stay at his joint after the hot reception I had just received. I think he cheated me a couple of hundreds on the rent, but I didn't care.

I'll tell you how I got to Frank's. I had worked my way into Baga beach slowly. Stopping at various places to inquire about the tariffs and generally getting a feel of the area. Touristy spots are notorious for ripping off people and I was wary. Passing up some fake smiles and a constant barrage of invitations, I finally landed on Frank's doorstep because he had a small enclosed yard where I could park my bike. Frank and his wife were sunning themselves in the yard. I was immediately offered a chair and a room. I was still being my cagey self and was talking around for a discount when the younger girl served me some water with a giggle. Then Jane, the older one, walked in and boldly demanded to know my name and where I came from. I gave her the details and she wanted to know about my journey. I told her it was a long story and she replied that there was plenty of time at the beach. She was wearing shorts with a brief, see-through halter.

Frank and his wife were enjoying the show. When I told them I'd been alone on the road for eight months, Jane couldn't believe it. And I couldn't believe her next question: '*What about women?*' I blushed and babbled foolishly, only to have persistent Jane repeat the question with a sexy shake of her boobs. At that point I requested to see the room on offer, just to avoid being grilled. The younger one took me on a recce, giggling all the while. She had a pert bottom, and she knew it, and she wanted me to appreciate it. Which I did with bulging eyes and drooling mouth. I hardly saw anything of the room, but I was hooked.

A cup of coffee was waiting for me with a cocksure Frank. Drinking coffee with Jane a foot away was unnerving. Frank's frank daughter was beginning to scare me with her brazenness. After a minute or so the inquisition started once more. This time, about the family, especially the wife. Was she pretty? How old was she? Where did she work? All the while the best angles of Jane were on exhibition. Or maybe my mind was working overtime. Two young, good-looking girls showering attention on me was a spectacular achievement. I revelled in that momentary happiness.

The girls took my bags to the room. I paid up and

Frank beamed with joy. To be fair to him, he hadn't asked for an advance, but I'd got into the habit of proffering one. The chatty girls were reluctant to leave the room and Jane washed my dirty clothes—for a fee, of course. I was to bump into them all over the place in the next three days.

Baga is one of the happening beaches at the moment. Full of Indian and foreign tourists. The young Indian couples are dressed snazzily and the women are wearing shorter clothes, and more and more Indian skin is on show. Just bummed around the beach with lots of beer in my beer belly. Ogling and leching is the done thing. A massage from a man from Hubli in Karnataka was nice. He told me—inevitably—his hard-luck story and I listened with half an ear. A ten-year-old girl performed some acrobatics and held out her hand for money. Some waiters argued for space on the beach and nearly came to blows. Some policemen were busy extracting money from the local businesses. Shakedowns by the police were a common sight all over India.

Beef curry, at an eatery just opposite Frank's hostelry, was a lethal-looking concoction but the taste was exquisite. The small tavern with an unkempt cook and a cocky waiter beckoned to me and on impulse, I entered the joint. Later in the day, as I once again espied Jane swing her way towards me, I dove into this joint again. The cocky waiter recommended the green beef curry, and I was a repeat guest. After a couple of days I was again eating the same thing when I noticed a lot of familiar faces. Some of them smiled at me, and then I caught on. All the guests around were waiters from the other restaurants. This was the waiters' watering-hole, and without the bow ties and the uniforms, they looked like tourists. No wonder the food was cheap and excellent, and the waiter was cocky. He must have thought I was just another waiter having a quick bite, and masquerading as a tourist. But my tip floored him and after that I was treated like royalty.

My torn saddlebag was repaired by a fast-talking conman who also happened to be a tailor working with leather. He stitched fawn-coloured leather onto my black canvas saddlebags and guaranteed a lifetime of rough use, or my money back. I had no choice but to allow myself to be conned, although I did not like his looks at all. I believed we shared a karmic history of dislike and violence. But I put aside the violence, contenting myself with mental epithets of almost equal malevolence.

It was a day to be conned, and I went into the shack of a palmist. His advertisement itself should have warned me. It said he knew yoga, reiki, palmistry, holistic healing (whatever that means), acupuncture, and God knows what else. A creepy fellow from the north, speaking his own version of English, with the mandatory long hair and beard, and festooned with necklaces. Thin as a reed, his forehead covered with ash, he was a caricature of a phoney fakir. Having dispatched his minion with leaflets announcing his achievements and talent, he turned his rheumy eyes on me with a viper's smile. He charged by the minute and he even had a stopwatch. He whispered that the charges had just gone up that very day and as proof he showed me his new leaflet. Time ticking on his side, he grabbed my hands and gazed at them with rapt attention, h'mm-ing for a long time. Minutes later I asked him to say something and he gave me the usual bullshit about the almost superman me, my godlike qualities too numerous to count. I may have enjoyed a prolonged shower of praise but for the stopwatch. I banged it shut and paid up.

Searching for a live band in the evening I came upon a two-man orchestra. The white singer was barely adequate, both at singing and at playing the guitar. His only qualifications seem to have been his colour and his ponytail. And the fact that he looked like Eric Clapton. The local drummer was loud and flashy. So I pepped up the evening by giving old Eric a complex with my talent in full flow. Lusty cheering from the crowd egged me on and for once I did not go overboard. At the right time I split the place after having gone into the women's bathroom by mistake. I picked up a sanitary disposal bag as a souvenir.

Pickled Parrot Four Seasons is a restaurant run by Jill, a sixty-year-old foreigner, probably British. I went there for a burger and she came out of the kitchen to ask me how I wanted it. She discussed the ingredients and I went along with her suggestions. It was a new experience for me to discuss a meal in such detail, including whether I wanted Italian or English mustard. I ate that burger with the respect that it deserved. There was a book in Jill's small library and I asked if I could purchase it. She sold it to me for eighty rupees. The same morning I was sold a second-hand book for two hundred rupees by a local fart. We Indians need to learn a thing or two from the whites.

I turned forty-four in Goa. Alone and feni-drunk. Feni is a dangerous drink, with a blinding hangover to follow. But Goa without feni is unthinkable. Many years ago I had nearly missed my flight out of Goa after a feni night. I was on the tarmac after the doors to the plane had been shut. The pilot took pity and let me in. That is what feni does to you. Feni did me in that night. Feni forty-four. Grabbed a song in the karaoke bar, was not appreciated by the crowd and went to sleep in a sulk. Happy birthday.

Frank and his crazy family turned out to wish me goodbye. I swear to God that Jane pinched my ass in farewell. Maybe I'd missed something there. The old white gay was still hanging around Baga beach, window-shopping for a partner. Maybe I'd missed something there, too.

35

A ride out from Goa is always a sad one. With a spectacular hangover it was even sadder. Bleary eyes and the stink of stale feni added to my misery. I wanted to be someone else today. Chugging along slowly, I saw a small dhaba near the border. *Pau bhaji with potato patties.* And dirt cheap too. The only way to fight a hangover is with food, in my case. So I made the dhaba-owner's day by gorging myself on most of his fare.

Four hundred-odd kilometres and I reached the outskirts of the small town of Mahad. Ravi's beer shop. Imagine, in the middle of nowhere, coming across a stand-alone shop offering umpteen varieties of beer. I screeched to a halt, taken in by the sight. Ravi was a talkative man with wagonloads of information about the place. We were in the district of Raigad, Chhatrapati Shivaji's bastion in the days gone by. Ravi is a proud Maharashtrian with, I was sure, political leanings towards the Shiv Sena. He lectured me on the problems in Maharashtra, surreptitiously opening bottles of Cobra beer as he spoke. I decided to spend the night at a hotel just a few yards from Ravi's beer parlour.

I got drunk. I am not a drunk but my halo had slipped two days in a row. I didn't realize how many sheets to the wind I was sailing till I stopped the bike at the hotel entrance and gently keeled over. Waiters came in droves to pick me and the bike up. Groups of families were eating inside and I felt them pulling their children closer to them. A terribly dirty drunk, when the night is still young, does not inspire confidence in young mothers—or young fathers for that matter. I swallowed my embarrassment and swaggered to the reception. A baleful chap asked me for an advance and looked surprised I had the money. After that I hid my head in the room.

Set out early the next morning to avoid the stares of just about everybody. I was striking out for Mumbai and wanted to get into the city early to locate my friend's pad. On the way I saw a car tailing me and the person driving the car was giving my gear the look-over properly. Then the chap gunned his motor, gave me a thumbs-up and disappeared from my life.

Two days on the Goa-Mumbai highway and I began to see the bored expressions of what I call the Bombay Barbies. These are women going for a holiday with their husbands and small kids. They are well groomed, wear huge dark glasses and pout a lot. Dozens of these zombies drifting by in their fancy cars. They didn't look too happy and I felt like screaming at them to get a life.

Mumbai was a bad dream. Even though I arrived early, I had to spend a lot of time looking for my actual destination. Since I didn't know the city at all, it was that much harder. I tried my luck with the autorickshaw-drivers. These are the worst of the thugs on Indian roads anywhere. I offered to pay them to guide me to my friend's home but was refused in quick succession by four of them. Hardened as I was to their tribe, I couldn't believe how churlish they were. Then I saw the light. They wanted to see cash up front. My appearance did not inspire fiscal confidence. I approached the fifth fellow with cash outstretched in my palm, and we had an immediate deal. Boy, my self-image took a beating. When the slime balls of the Indian roads don't trust you, you have a problem with your looks.

Karden Denjongpa is an old friend of Sikkimese origin. She works as a stewardess with Air India. I found her flat, and her, and made myself at home. I met her flatmate, Kesang. It was nice to be served by two classy air-hostesses, especially after the characters who'd administered to me on the road. These girls had just got back from home and I was blessed with all the goodies from there. Pork, dried beef, special round chillies and our local cheese, made my day. I desperately needed a bath and asked if I could have one. The bathroom was laid open to me with accompanying toilet rules and regulations. No slippers allowed, all footwear outside the bathroom on a special mat, etc. I did not bother with the rules and nearly lost a gracious hostess. I found it necessary to learn the hang of things around the house quickly.

The girls were not married and had been living by their own rules for decades. Set way of doing things. We crammed for a night in the single-bedroom flat. I got the bed and they got the sofas. I also got a few mosquitoes. City-bred mosquitoes are clearly more vicious and definitely smarter than their country cousins. I was supposed to stay for a day or two but the cramped quarters weren't conducive to lazing around in. Despite Dr Yeller's medicine, I was having a horrible time with my fingers. Arthritic fingers on a motorcycle ride are not exactly a pleasure. I was also feeling travel fatigue and wanted to conclude the journey as quickly as possible.

So I went to visit Andy and his NGO in Thane, on my way out towards Vadodara. Andy is from a missionary family from America, married to an Indian. They are doing sterling work for HIV/AIDS patients. I was given breakfast by him and was about to start eating when I sensed the shocked looks of the entire family. The egg was halfway to my mouth when I hurriedly put it down. Grace was to be said first. Andy prayed with a fervour I've rarely witnessed at a breakfast. He literally talked to God, and there I was, squirming at my social gaffe. Andy speaks softly, with a special shine to his blue eyes, and before long he was passionately expounding on his work and his religion. His two small kids put up an impromptu small show with hymns as the centre-piece. I was taken to their clinic where there was a reading of the Bible and some more hymns. A power-point presentation of their activities followed. The final goodbye was with Andy clutching my hands on the street with a prayer. I have never prayed so much in such a short time. They were friends of my missionary sister and she'd wanted me to visit them. I did not regret the visit but I was overwhelmed by the praying.

The Mumbai-Vadodara highway has the highest volume of traffic in India. I must have crossed thousands of vehicles that day. Traffic was choked for kilometres on end, with the expansion of the road underway. The 'dustbath' was an unending affair and I went off the road several times to escape the jam. Some God-forsaken small town was to be my night halt but the room was terribly dirty. The waiter was a toughie and tried to almost bully me into staying in the room. He insisted that the bedsheets were clean—an outright lie—and I nearly hit him in the face. During the entire journey this was the closest I got to violence. Only my size and menacing demeanour kept him in check, the insolent bugger. Reached Vadodara with crackers bursting and streets filled with smog.

Alex from England, and I, landed up at the hotel at the same time. We got to talking at the reception. He had been loafing all over India for the past three months and had been in Goa at the same time that I was there. We were bound to meet, said some deep logic of the universe. I treated him to some really inferior biryani. He looked emaciated and gobbled up the food. I think he was on a one-meal-a-day trip. This mason from England looked like a tramp and I wondered why he was punishing himself so much. If he kept this up much longer, he would die. I could not resist telling him to go home. He took the unsolicited advice with good humour and promised to go back soon.

Bacchu bhai is a roadside tea-vendor and poor as can be. But he is a Hindu zealot with a political stand as clear as day. He assumed I was another zealot and was travelling around India with the sole purpose of visiting temples. I did nothing to dispel that notion. In fact I was back to my favourite pastime of putting my imagination to some heavy work. I did not lie about the temples. I had visited many of them over the years and gave him a first-hand account of Sabarimala, and the Guruvayoor temple of Kerala. I got a cup of tea and a cigarette free from Bacchu for my tales. Being nice to pilgrims was a religious act for him.

Rajasthan is a massive state with long unpopulated stretches. I did not get enough to eat that day. Just some tea and biscuits. The countryside is hot and arid but beautiful. After more than 600 kilometres, I landed in Beawar. I found the people of the region simple, with an innate sense of hospitality. My hands were killing me and I could not even write my notes for the night. I decided to end the journey and head for Delhi for a week's rest, before returning to Rajasthan, and Jaipur, to attend a course in Vipassana.

Arriving in Delhi the next day, and finally hanging up my boots, was a relief and a regret at the same time.

Constant movement can become addictive and, when the constant traveller is deprived of it, he tends to miss the chance encounters with those highly individualistic characters on the road. But my age had finally caught up with me and I had to bail out a month before I had planned to.

Dicky and Ramesh were, as always, ready with a welcome smile. To celebrate the formal end to my trip, we cracked open a bottle of the finest and got properly sloshed. My journey was not yet over, however. After the course in meditation, I had to find a place to write in, with Vijay's help.

Till then, lazing around was blissful. The swollen fingers got their well-deserved rest and attention and Dr Yeller's oil was applied on them in copious quantities. I derived the hugest pleasure in meeting old friends and boasting about my accomplishment. Wherever I went, I was met by the jealous stares of men and the fluttering eyelashes of admiring women.

36

Govind Mohan is the quintessential bureaucrat. A good friend of mine and a fellow meditator. I took a ride with him to Jaipur where we would be meditating for ten days. Govind even looks like a bureaucrat, with the dead serious expression, slow, deliberate movement, the mandatory pair of thick plastic glasses and the controlled laugh patented by bureaucrats all over the world. His smile is only fleeting, and I long to see him guffaw just once.

On the road to Jaipur I grew quickly reacquainted with the comforts of an air-conditioned car. Govind regaled me with gossip about my old cronies. He also came up with the profound statement that we Indians should put sex behind us and get on with our lives. Perhaps the Government of India has checked the Internet sites visited by babus, and found those dealing with porn at the top of the heap.

About sixty of us had registered for the course. The

first day went in familiarizing ourselves with the rules and regulations, and the place itself. Rooms were allotted and we were not to speak to anyone but our Teacher or the management for the next nine-and-a-half days.

Three days were spent in learning a system of meditation called *ana-pana*, which is an exercise in improving concentration on the natural flow of breath through the nostrils. Vipassana was taught on the fourth day, focusing on the sensations of the body, the ultimate goal being enlightenment. There were recorded discourses at the end of each day by Shree S.N. Goenkaji, encapsulating the lessons of the day, with some advice for the morrow. The regimen was strenuous. The wake-up call came at four in the morning, and practice began in half an hour. Breakfast was a simple meal at 6.30, followed by further meditation, and lunch at 11.30. Senior students did not have dinner, which was served to the rest at 5.30 p.m. We got to bed by around 9.30. There were a few breaks in between, but most of the time was spent in the meditation hall. The food was wholesome and vegetarian. There are no charges for the course, but voluntary donations are accepted at the end of it.

I feel I should describe some of my fellow inmates, but since there is complete segregation of the sexes I can only talk about the males.

I have to start with a monk in saffron robes who, being a member of the Sangha, was granted an elevated seat even though he was a first-time student of the present technique of meditation. This gentleman, gaining comfort from our silent familiarity by the third day, started to pass gas with amazing frequency, and at full volume. I had never heard such shameless farting in a roomful of people who were not related to each other. Perhaps he considered us family. He was a diminutive man, necessarily quiet, but capable of booming sound from an entirely wrong aperture.

Then there was the ego freak, considered the seniormost among us for having done the most number of courses. As an assertion of his superiority, he made it a point to be the last to enter the hall, just seconds before the Teacher. He was generally among the first, however, to enter the dining room, where he consumed obscene amounts of food. I also saw him admiring himself in the mirrors at various urinals on the campus.

But he hadn't contended with the Ninja. The Ninja came a day late and forced his way to a front-row seat with us seniors. He was an Israeli, wearing baggy Afghan trousers and a scarf perpetually wrapped around his face. He supplemented his diet by eating some sort of organic health paste. He had the quaint habit of blessing his food with the palms of both his hands before he ate. He gave the ego freak cause for competition by beating him by nanoseconds to be the last one to enter the meditation hall. To be fair to the Ninja, he was a serious meditator, except for his well-timed entrance.

Govind looked deadly serious throughout, as if the balance of the country's payments was his immediate concern. He walked with a measured tread, hands always behind his back, to sit royally on the bench in the middle of the park, looking like a district collector waiting for the peon to bring in the files. He had a bureaucratic friend who was the only one who dressed formally for meditation, right down to his meticulous black leather shoes. During breaks he could be seen walking around at a furious pace, going nowhere. Definitely a government servant.

Then there were the two perverts—one Indian and the other American. The Indian used to stand watching at a point from where you could see a part of the women's entrance through the surrounding foliage. He would pretend to exercise and twirl his arms around, all the while keeping his neck and head ramrod straight. He would have been a cricket commentator's delight. The American was a good-looking, long-haired fellow with gigolo written all over him. He could be found jostling for space with the Indian pervert. The evening discourse in English was in a smaller hall, where the women joined us, and our man would be staring at the ladies the whole time. I know, because my seat was right behind him.

Jeff, a Canadian carpenter, rode a bike to the retreat. A tall, lanky, man with a greying ponytail, he brought in a special stool to meditate on. He also stood on a cushion to survey the Teacher's seat. We later saw him walking around with his fingers in a certain sutra position. Jeff had learnt a variety of meditation techniques from all over the world, and he was mixing things up.

Another ten-day course began as ours ended, and I got to talking to Peter, from Holland. A sixty-year-old with a phenomenal record in essays in faith. He had done the ten-day course twenty-two times, the seven-day *satti pathan* course eighteen times and the thirty-day course five times over. Spent his life just chasing the sun. Claimed to be a poet whose verses were read out on the local radio back in his Dutch hometown. I surmised he came from a rich family and did not have to work for a living. Lucky sod.

At the end of my course, I was reluctant to leave the place. Dhamma Thali Vipassana Centre is a beautiful piece of property on the outskirts of Jaipur. It is well managed and runs like clockwork. There are so many peacocks and other birds to see that at times it feels like an aviary. People lose a lot of pent-up grief when they go there. You see them coming out looking lighter, younger, slimmer. Even their complexions clear up.

As I write this down in Begnass I marvel at the fact that the Pokhra chapter of the Vipassana Centre is just visible from where I stay. It is in the process of being built, and they are already holding a ten-day 'gypsy camp' course with minimal infrastructure. I just heard the registration day dinner bell go. How is that for connections of the karmic variety?

The Dhamma Sikkim Centre started functioning when a few of us got together to give a fillip to the practice of meditation for laymen. Within a space of seven to eight years we now have an active organization with regular courses being held and hundreds of practitioners in the state.

What vipassana has taught me is to react less emotionally to negative forces. In the past, when anger or hurt assailed me, I would roll in misery for days on end, plotting grizzly revenge on their cause. Now, I'm lot more detached. Without vipassana training I would never have left the IAS, and would still be howling at the moon over my fate.

37

Hitched a ride with Govind till the outskirts of Delhi where I was picked up by Arvind, an old college friend. Arvind looks like Shakti Kapoor, the popular casting choice for a villain in Hindi movies, the only difference being, Arvind looks more vicious. Arvind had studied at another college, but we had drugs in common. He would sidle in quietly into my room and wait for his turn at the orgy. I don't know when I started on brown sugar but I was a heavy smoker by my third year in college. I had experimented with lots of drugs and settled in for a long-term affair with heroin. Arvind was my local contact and we used to go pretty far in search of the stuff, sometimes travelling to Delhi's satellite towns in train box-cars.

We'd been caught by the police on many occasions and hauled off to different cop stations where I would claim to be 'Yogdeep Gurung from Kirorimal College, room number 117'. This was standard drill. After dire threats and a shakedown we were always let off, with a warning. I imagine the cops had little paperwork to spare on college kids out for a good time. I told Yogdeep about my subterfuge two decades after we were done with college and the bugger confessed he'd used my name and hostel room number for the same purpose. We deserved each other as friends.

Arvind's house was just behind the campus and I was a regular pile-on for meals at his house. Somehow, I'd kept my grades in college at first-division level and this used to impress his mother no end, leading her to believe I was his only 'clean' friend. So food was plentiful at his house, accompanied by a warm welcome to their table every time.

Another regularly crazed-out character was Narayan, alias Peter, a Bihari born and brought up in Sikkim. When his money came in from home at the beginning of each month, he would disappear for a week, treating girls to movies and the like. For the remaining three weeks he would beg around for cigarettes and cups of tea. He took a girl out to a discotheque once, and after a single dance, led her to the railway station. There, she had to make do with a cup of tea till morning as he had run out of money. He never saw her again.

Arvind had been lost to me for more than twenty years. Two weeks after I had resigned my job, he called up. It was like a voice from the dead. He is now a married man, with a child, and plays the stock market in partnership with his younger sister Guddi, who used to serve me food in the old days. I perceived the sudden reappearance of my friend at this juncture as a cosmic tie-up. We may even end up setting up a business together.

Arvind greeted me on the crossroads with a hug, and we zoomed to his house in Faridabad. I got a lecture from his parents for not keeping in touch over the years. I deserved that.

Sikkim, for a few restful days back home, and then on to Kathmandu, with my younger daughter Dechen for company this time. We halted at my cousins', and after paying homage to Joey, of 'kitchen cuddle' fame, we arrived in Pokhra. Three days in Vijay's house convinced me I would not be able to write a word there. His place, with the daily parties that lasted till the sun came up, provided no fertile ground for contemplation, and I told him as much. A brilliant thought struck him and he took me to see the lake-side property in Begnass the same day. An hour's ride from Pokhra, we hit the steep dirt road and entered a dark forest with a slippery path through it. The forest opened suddenly onto open plateau on which sat a picture-book cottage with stone benches overlooking the lake and the Annapurna range. I was already in love with the place. Forest all around, with the nearest house at least 200 metres away. I was a goner.

I was introduced to the lazy god, who had found the

time and energy to produce a large family. Seven kids, with one dead; total at hand, six. They were to be my family for more than two months.

The cottage had been bought from the original owner and minimally touched up by the Shangri-La Group of hotels. So I enjoyed only the most basic facilities that came with it. No attached toilet and no running hot water. I missed the presence of neither a gas range, nor television. Firewood amply did the job of cooking and heating, and the family and their antics were my soap opera for the evenings. It was normal for there to be no electricity for as long as eleven hours in a day. Evenings were spent around a campfire, before I retired from the scene to write by candlelight.

Fifty-two-year-old Mohan was short, thin and dark, with a pleasant face and a wide smile, and a penchant for gambling. He spoke the formal Nepali of the elite, and was ready to do anything—that is, in principle. Action seldom evolved from his honeyed words. He barked orders to his family but no one paid much heed to them.

We agreed that he would provide us two meals a day on a budget of Rs 4,000 a month. I gave him an advance of Rs 2,000 and grand feasting followed. Chicken and fish abounded in the fare. My caution to him to go easy on the meat fell on deaf ears. Within a week we were reduced to one vegetable and rice with a watery daal on the table. He ran out of funds with furious speed, and I began to dread his early morning visits, when he invariably asked for more. A cup of tea served by his hands usually cost me two to five hundred rupees. Fed up of being haunted by Mohan, I called him to my room one day and gave him hell. I shoved five thousand rupees in his hand and told him that would be the last of the money he would get from me till I left. Joy to the world. Chicken that same night at the top of the menu.

On the flipside, he was a gentleman with an immense heart. He was always gentle with his kids and their friends. He loved animals. A black kitten left by others to die found a home with him. He shared his food with his two dogs. And he was immensely popular. Going to the small town of Begnass with him was like following a top-notch politician on a campaign trail. A shouted greeting here, a hello there, a backslap to a pal, a quick flirtatious interlude with the women. He was vain about his appearance and preened a good deal in front of his huge elaborate mirror, the only item of worth in his house.

The mother of the house was a rough-cut village woman apologetic about her rustic speech. She had some kind of skin disease and was conscious about it. She looked depressed in the mornings and would not come near me. Evenings by the firelight she would be peppy and garrulous. After a week I realized it was alcohol that made the difference. She was an advanced alcoholic, her litany of woes topped by the inferior man she had married. But they were a happy couple, in the end. They even shared cigarettes. Mohan was an expert at filching cigarettes, candles and soap from me. Sometimes, I felt like I was living in a college hostel all over again.

The eldest son was something else. I could barely resist kicking him in the backside. Working as a fabricator, he contributed nothing, absolutely nothing, to the home fires. The son of a bitch used to come home around 5.30 in the evening only to grab his food and split from there. Some of my money went his way, too, when his parents refused to pay for his meals.

Manoj was the second son and the backbone of the house. He was the donkey, the firewood collector, the cook, the farmer and the coolie of the family. He became my valet, too, in a way. Manoj was too serious for his age, which was twenty-one. But with an eighteen-year-old father, had he a choice but to age quickly?

Chija, the eldest daughter, was the other slave of the family. Carrying drinking water home on her back, cutting the grass and washing clothes were her primary duties. At nineteen, in the rural world she should have been a mother of two, at least. But she remains a kid at heart, with no interest in boys, as far as I could perceive.

I met the third son only once since he was away on work. He once wanted his sisters to take flowers to a girl on Valentine's Day. His request, over the village telephone, was discussed threadbare at the campfire board meeting and rejected as being too expensive and unnecessary.

The second girl was with us for two weeks only, after she ran away from the house where she was staying and working. A smart female of sixteen, she will run away again one of these days.

The youngest, also a girl, Aarti, has a mind equally of

her own. Only twelve years old, she loafs about the village all the time she isn't in school. Always ready for a fight, she will choose a life of excitement and end up doing well for herself.

Mohan and his largely peaceful family taught me a thing or two. I had never lived in such close quarters with poor people. There was never enough at home, and still less to entertain friends on. Among these people, nobody expected food at another's home. When I invited some of their visitors to eat what was at home, they declined politely. But they contrived to party all the same. There may not have been anything to eat, but some local liquor was served and there was singing and dancing. The lady of the house would sing in her lovely voice, and Mohan's madal would provide the percussion.

I may have issues with my life, and I have been buffeted about a bit, but those are nothing compared to the daily battering taken by Mohan and his ilk. Living with them has made me rethink many established idiocies and realize that all those high-sounding spiritual, psychological and emotional arguments we have the luxury to engage in, in our temperature-controlled drawing rooms, take a very low backseat indeed when you are existing— *subsisting*—day to day.

Look at me. It's just getting to be a year since I rendered myself jobless, and the cowries from my retirement bonus have long run out. But I'd had a blast of a year, hadn't I. And, far from starving, I feel richer than—I'll bet—most of you do. You and I have Thamzi, mate, like it or not. Catch up with it any time you like.

We'll be waiting.

Thamzi and I.